A GENTLEMAN IN LOVE

Thalia walked slowly across the lawn, through the rose garden, to the lily pond. "It is a place for lovers," she thought instinctively. Then she drew her breath as if the thought stabbed her like a sharp dagger.

"You are not crying, Thalia?" came an unexpected voice. It was the Earl, standing beside her, his grey eyes holding her captive. Then he pulled her into his arms, holding her close against him. She was trembling with the ecstasy he had evoked in her and she thought he was trembling too.

Then he was kissing her wildly, passionately, and a fire leapt within them both, until Thalia seemed to break under the strain of it and she hid her face against his shoulder.

"How soon will you marry me?" he asked at last.

Bantam Books by Barbara Cartland
Ask your bookseller for the books you have missed

Barbara Cartland's Library of Love series

Books of Love and Revelation

Other Books by Barbara Cartland

A Gentleman in Love

Barbara Cartland

A GENTLEMAN IN LOVE
A Bantam Book / February 1980

ISBN 0-553-13447-7

Published simultaneously in the United States and Canada

Bantam Books are published by Bantam Books, Inc. Its trademark, consisting of the words "Bantam Books" and the por-
trayal of a bantam, is Registered in U.S. Patent and Trademark
Office and in other countries. Marca Registrada. Bantam
Books, Inc., 666 Fifth Avenue, New York, New York 10019.

PRINTED IN THE UNITED STATES OF AMERICA

DESIGNED BY MIERRE

Author's Note

Duels of honour were private encounters about real or imagined insults. Duels with swords spread over Europe from Italy at the end of the Fifteenth Century. In France, political duels were frequent in the nineteenth Century and took place occasionally in the Twentieth.

In England, famous duels were those between Lord Castlereagh and George Canning in 1809, and between the Duke of Wellington and the tenth Earl of Winchelsea in 1829. In 1881, an act making duelling a military affair resulted in duels being fought abroad at Calais or Boulogne.

Hatchard's Book-Shop still exists today at 190 Piccadilly.

Chapter One

1815

"I see nothing in this that is remarkable," the Honourable Richard Rowlands said, inspecting his newly tied cravat from every angle.

"There is a difference, Sir," his valet said respectfully.

"Well, to me it looks just a muddle," Richard Rowlands said disagreeably.

"I agree with you," said a voice from the doorway.

The Honourable Richard swung round with an exclamation.

"Vargus! I did not know you had returned to London!"

"I arrived late last night," the Earl of Hellington replied, "and I broke my own record, as I intended."

"With new horses?"

"With the chestnuts I bought at Tattersall's when you were with me."

"I thought they would prove outstanding," Richard Rowlands said. "Sit down, Vargus, and have a glass of champagne, or would you prefer brandy?"

"It is too early in the day for either," the Earl answered, "but I would like a cup of coffee."

1

His friend made a face.

"Beastly stuff except when one wants to keep awake."

"I thought you had more alluring attractions to do that for you," the Earl remarked mockingly.

As he spoke, he sat down in a comfortable armchair and crossed his legs, his polished Hessians with their gold tassels shining in a manner which brought a look of admiration into the valet's eyes as he moved from the room to fetch the coffee the Earl preferred.

Richard Rowlands made no effort to continue dressing but turned round to sit in his shirt-sleeves, looking his friend over critically.

"You look damned well!" he said. "I suppose it is the country air."

"I have been out in all weathers, training a new horse with which I intend to win every steeple-chase in the County," the Earl replied.

"You always do," Richard said laconically, "and it is not surprising, considering you always have the best horses because you train them yourself."

"That is the secret, my dear Richard," the Earl said. "If you stopped chasing women and concentrated on horses, you would find yourself a better equestrian and very much better in health."

His friend gave a laugh.

"At the moment, the only thing I could afford to train would be a mule for which no-one else had any use."

"Under the hatches?" the Earl asked sympathetically.

"Completely," Richard replied, "and this time I cannot turn to my father for assistance. He swore to me when I went to him six months ago that he would never bail me out again, and he said that as far as he was concerned I could stay in the Fleet until I rotted!"

"Strong words!" the Earl remarked. "But of course I will see that that does not happen to you."

"No, Vargus. It is very decent of you to suggest it," Richard protested, "but you know I swore when we first became friends that I would not sponge on you as three-quarters of your acquaintances manage to do, and it is a vow I intend to keep."

"It is easy to be proud—if you can afford it," the Earl said cynically.

"Well, I cannot afford it, but I am still proud."

"In which case," the Earl replied, "I hope you will find it edible. I have no wish ever again to be as hungry as we were sometimes with Wellington's Army. I remember several occasions when I was so empty I would gladly have eaten my boots."

"I am not likely to forget that," Richard agreed. "But if we start talking about the war I shall forget everything else. Why are you back in London?"

The Earl hesitated and his friend looked at him in surprise.

Ever since they had served in the same Regiment they had been such close friends that Richard believed they had no secrets from each other.

When the war was over, they both turned spontaneously to the gaieties of London as a relief from the privations and discomforts they had suffered in Portugal and Spain.

Even so, when reminiscing they had found it easier to remember the glory and the triumph.

But Waterloo had not only brought the cessation of hostilities with the French, it had also brought young men back into civilian life with not enough to do except seek enjoyment.

This was not difficult in the case of the Earl, who was an exceedingly wealthy man, but dozens of his contemporaries like Richard Rowlands found themselves with a champagne taste but unable to afford anything but home-brewed ale, unless they were prepared to run into debt.

The Regent had set the fashion for extravagance and the amassing of pile upon pile of unpaid bills, which was being emulated in an alarming fashion by the friends he entertained at Carlton House.

When they were not there, they frequented the Clubs in St. James's Street.

There they would gamble with what ready money they could find and discuss the merits of the latest social "Incomparable" and the fascination of the "Impures" who were to be found in the Theatres and the dance-halls at which they were always welcome.

Despite the restrictions imposed upon him by the narrowness of his purse, Richard Rowlands had enjoyed not only the night-life of London but the race-meetings, the Mills, the horse-sales, and every other event to which the *Beaux* and the Dandies flocked daily.

He had thought that the Earl was as fascinated as he was by every new excitement, so he was extremely surprised when three weeks ago he had suddenly and for no apparent reason left London for his country house in Kent.

He gave no explanation for his decision except that he had things to see to in the country.

Richard had missed the Earl more than he would admit, and had waited expectantly for an invitation to Hellington Park, only to be disappointed.

Now the Earl was back, and he said impatiently:

"Come on, Vargus! It is not like you to be mysterious. If it is a woman who is coming between us, I swear I shall feel like throttling her!"

"It is not any particular woman, yet in a way you are being clairvoyant, except that the woman you wish to throttle has, as yet, no name."

"What the devil do you mean by that?" Richard enquired.

As he spoke, his valet came back into the room with a tray on which were a silver coffee-pot, a cream-jug, and a large, man-sized cup.

4

He set it down on a small table by the Earl, who thanked him.

When he left the room, the Earl said:

"I went to the country, Richard, to think."

"To think?" his friend exclaimed.

He spoke incredulously, as if he had never heard of the exercise.

"I thought," he continued after a moment, "that you were finding Lady Adelaide rather a bore. At the same time, that little dancer—what was her name? Fay?—was divinely alluring."

"I paid her off," the Earl said.

"You got rid of her?" Richard asked. "For whom?"

There was a pause before the Earl replied:

"I do not know yet, but I have decided I shall get married."

"Who is to be the fortunate bride?"

"As I say, I have not yet found her."

Richard gave a laugh.

"That is just like you, Vargus! You make up your mind about something and plan it out like a military campaign. Well, I think you are wise, in your position, to marry. It is obvious that you need an heir, but for God's sake choose the right woman, or it will not be I who will throttle her but you!"

"That is exactly what I thought myself," the Earl replied seriously.

He took a sip of coffee before he went on:

"I went to Hellington because I felt stifled in London and bored with the endless gambling and drinking and having to toady to all those fat women at Carlton House."

Richard laughed.

"I agree with you. Lady Hertford ruins one's enjoyment of the time one spends there, but I am genuinely fond of Prinny."

"So am I," the Earl agreed. "But he has become too pompous lately and far too sensitive about himself. I suppose we can thank Beau Brummell for that."

Both men were silent for a moment, knowing that because Beau Brummell had insulted the Heir to the Throne by calling him fat, it had made him long avidly for personal compliments in a manner which his friends often found disconcerting.

"Whatever else Prinny is," the Earl said, "he has excellent taste. In fact, it is outstanding except where it concerns his women!"

"I believe things were much better when he was with Mrs. Fitzherbert," Richard replied, "although I am too young to remember."

"So am I," the Earl agreed.

"Now, let me think . . ." Richard said, "you are just a year older than I, which means you will be twenty-eight this year. It is certainly time you married, Vargus. Most men of your consequence are married off almost as soon as they leave Oxford."

"When I was that age," the Earl said, "I suppose my choice would have been confined to either a Portuguese peasant or one of those aggressive camp followers who followed the Army. They would hardly grace my table at Hellington."

"That is true," Richard said with a smile. "And I have always believed that a wife is a very different 'kettle of fish' from the Ladies of Fashion who have a 'come hither' look in their eyes almost before you are introduced."

"That is exactly what I think myself," the Earl said, "and while I know exactly what you are hinting at, Richard, I have no intention of marrying Lady Adelaide or any woman in the least like her."

There was a smile of satisfaction on Richard's face as he thought of the dark-haired, tempestuous "Incomparable" who had been pursuing the Earl ever since he had appeared in London.

She was beautiful and undoubtedly alluring in

a serpentine manner that made her the centre of the social scene, despite the fact that she was rivalled by Lady Caroline Lamb, who was notoroious for her mad infatuation for Lord Byron, and by a number of other beauties who dispensed their favours very generously on those they fancied.

Lady Adelaide was a widow and had made no secret of her determination to marry the Earl.

If Richard had been surprised at his friend's sudden disappearance to the country, Lady Adelaide had made no pretence of not being disconsolate.

"Go and fetch him back, Richard," she had said at the last party at which they had met, and there had been no need for her to explain to whom she was referring.

"Vargus will return when he is ready to do so," Richard had replied defiantly.

Lady Adelaide put her hand on his arm and looked up at him with an expression in her eyes which she knew could send a man crazy with desire.

"Do it for me, dearest Richard," she said. "You know I would not be—ungrateful."

For a moment she had almost hypnotised him into agreeing to do anything she asked. Then he shook himself free and said:

"I have no more influence over Vargus than you have. If he wishes to return, he will do so. If not, he will stay away."

It was true that the Earl was a law unto himself.

He was used to commanding, used to being obeyed. Wellington had said that he found him an exceptional leader of men for the simple reason that he made up his mind what he wanted and could never visualise for a moment that he would not attain it.

Looking at him now, Richard thought that while

7

it would be easy for him to get any woman he desired, she would be taking on a very hard task in trying to be the wife he wanted.

For one thing, he would expect perfection—nothing else was acceptable where the Earl was concerned.

Thinking over the women he knew, Richard could not think of one who qualified for that requirement.

As if he realised what his friend was thinking, the Earl said:

"It will not be easy. When I looked at Hellington, which has been somewhat neglected since the war, I was aware it needed a woman's presence and something else which only she could give it."

"What is that?" Richard enquired.

"It should be a home," the Earl said. "That is what it meant to me when I was a boy, and I know that it now lacks something—I suppose you could call it 'atmosphere.' "

"I think I understand what you are trying to say," Richard answered. "I felt the same when my mother died. The house seemed empty."

"Exactly!" the Earl said. "And also, if I do not get the heir you suggest, the next in line for the title is an uncle who is unmarried, and after him another uncle whom I have never cared for, with only four daughters."

"Good God!" Richard exclaimed. "You will certainly have to get busy to prevent a succession of that sort!"

The Earl drank some more coffee, then said:

"I came back to London to find a pile of invitations waiting for me. There are a number from women who, I believe, are introducing their daughters to Society. I thought you and I might go along to one or two of them."

Richard gave a groan and said:

8

"I cannot imagine anything more depressing. Have you ever been to one of those Balls where young girls predominate? It is about a thousand times more formal and more boring than Almack's."

"That is what I suspected," the Earl said, "but the only alternative is to ask someone like Lady Melbourne to introduce me to the right sort of young woman. And look what happened to George Byron."

As he spoke, he was thinking of how disastrous Lord Byron's marriage had been and how Lady Byron, now that he had gone abroad, was working up a case for divorce, with details of cruelty and infidelity which were making the scandal-mongers lick their lips.

"I am not going to have that sort of thing happening," the Earl went on firmly. "I will choose my own wife and I will have no meddlesome interference."

"She will have to be of the highest breeding," Richard said. "After all, your mother was the Duke of Dorset's daughter, and no-one gives himself more airs than the present Duke."

He paused, then added quickly in case the Earl should think he was criticising:

"And quite rightly. The Dorsets were never part of the Carlton House Set. At least, that is what my father told me."

"It is true," the Earl replied, "and I certainly would not allow my mother's place to be filled by any doxy. At the same time, to be truthful, I find a lot of my Dorset relations extremely dull. They have allied themselves with the King and Queen and spend most of their time decrying the morals, manners, and extravagances of our friend Prinny."

"And of quite a lot of other people as well," Richard added, "but that is the sort of background your future wife must come from."

The Earl put down his cup with a little clatter.

9

"In books it is always so easy," he said. "The hero meets the heroine, they fall in love, he turns out to be a Prince in disguise and she is not the 'goose-girl' but the daughter of a King."

Richard drew back his head and laughed.

"Where on earth have you heard such stories?"

The Earl laughed too.

"My first Governess, who used to read to me fairy-stories every night before I went to sleep, was an incurable romantic. I suppose because children are impressionable, I remember those fairy-stories when I have forgotten a whole number of other, much more important things."

"You will have to see that your children are brought up from a very early age on historical facts and philosophy."

"It is no use telling me what I should do with my children until I have them, and before I have children I have to find a wife! Come on, Richard, help me! You are not being very constructive."

"Ever since I have known you," Richard replied, "you have always set me impossible tasks. I remember at Eton you used to demand delicacies that were out of season and quite unobtainable within the School bounds. When we were in the Army, I was sent foraging when there was not a pig or a chicken within a hundred miles of where we were camped. And now I have to find you a wife!"

He threw up his hands and exclaimed:

"Dammitall, Vargus, it is far simpler to provide you with a dozen doxies of the first water!"

"I can find those myself," the Earl replied.

"That reminds me," Richard said, "I promised to look in on Genevieve this morning. If you have not met her, it is something which definitely should be a part of your education."

"Who is Genevieve?" the Earl asked, without much interest in his voice.

10

"She is the latest addition to Madam Vestris's ballet at the King's Theatre."

"I have met Madam, and although her legs are exceptional, she is too flamboyant for my taste," the Earl remarked.

He was speaking of the dazzling young actress who, it had been said, "sang like an angel, danced like a sylph, and possessed the most shapely legs in the world."

"I agree with you," Richard said, "but Genevieve is different. She only arrived from France about a fortnight ago—in fact, just after you left—and she has taken London by storm."

"I seem to have heard that story before."

"I know, Vargus, but she really is exceptional. She not only dances well, but she has a charm which does not come off with the grease-paint. Come and meet her, and you will see that I am not exaggerating."

"I will come," the Earl replied, "if you promise to accompany me to at least two of the Balls which are taking place tonight."

Richard groaned, and the Earl added:

"One of them will not be too bad, because it is at Ashburnham House."

"The Princess de Lievens!" Richard exclaimed. "At least she introduced us to the waltz, even though she has the sharpest tongue that ever graced an Embassy."

The Earl laughed.

"She is too clever to cause a diplomatic incident, but I often wonder how long it will be before the Russian Ambassador is recalled."

"He will not be, if his wife can prevent it. The Princess likes England—or should I say the English."

Richard rose to his feet as he spoke and shouted for his valet.

"Jarvis!"

The man came hurrying into the room to help him into the exceedingly smart cut-away coat with long tails which, because it fitted without a wrinkle, had obviously been made by Weston.

"You will find that the Princess will be only too willing to assist you in your search, Vargus," Richard remarked.

As he spoke, there was a twinkle in his eye as if he knew he was being provocative.

"I have already told you, I will have no interference from women of any sort," the Earl replied, "and everything I have said to you, Richard, is of course in confidence. If you betray me, I swear I will call you out!"

Richard laughed.

"Since you are a far better shot than I am, it would be sheer murder, and you would have to flee the country. After all those years in the Peninsula, I suspect you have had enough of foreign parts."

"I certainly have!" the Earl said fervently. "Quite frankly, Richard, I am glad to be home. But there is a devil of a lot to do."

He gave a sigh.

"The people I employ have grown old, the Estate has been neglected, and because everyone was concentrating on the war, there have been practically no repairs done on the houses, barns, fences, or anything else."

"That should keep you busy," Richard remarked. "But enough, you are depressing me! Come on, Vargus! Let us go and call on Genevieve."

"I am not certain I feel very friendly towards French women at the moment," the Earl commented.

His friend laughed.

"Does it matter what her nationality is, as long as she is attractive? And let me assure you that French women, like French wines, are, I find, far more delectable than the English variety."

Carrying his hat and cane, Richard started to

walk down the stairs of his lodgings as he spoke, and the Earl, smiling, followed him.

Outside the house in Half Moon Street there was an exceedingly smart Phaeton drawn by two superfine horses.

Richard glanced at them with a touch of envy in his eyes before he climbed into the seat beside the Earl.

A groom wearing the Hellington livery released the horses' heads, and as the Phaeton moved off, he ran to spring up into the small seat behind the Earl and his friend.

Driving with an expertise that had made him in the short time he had been back in England an acclaimed "Corinthian," the Earl turned into Piccadilly.

A number of people walking along the pavement stopped to stare at the arresting picture he made with the smartness of his Phaeton, his horses, and of course himself.

With his tall hat at exactly the right angle on his dark hair, the Earl drew the eyes of every woman within a small radius and appeared supremely unaware that their hearts beat quicker at the mere sight of him.

If there was one thing he disliked, it was a reference to his looks, and he had already threatened to thrash any man who spoke of him as a "Beau."

"It is only a fashionable term," Richard protested.

"I do not care! It is insulting for any man to be called beautiful, or for that matter a 'Dandy,' and it is certainly not the way I wish to be described."

Richard had teased him but had been too wise to use the term himself.

He was well aware that although the Earl kept his temper under control, he had one, and he had no wish to have it expended upon him personally.

They drove along Piccadilly towards the King's Theatre, which was situated in the Haymarket.

"If your French woman is as attractive as you describe," the Earl said, "she does not live in a very salubrious neighbourhood."

As he spoke, they were passing through the dusty streets round the Theatre, which in the winter were a quagmire of mud.

"She has, wisely, not been in a hurry to make her choice of a protector," Richard replied quickly, "well aware that she will have a large number of applicants for the position."

"Which you are thinking might include me?" the Earl questioned.

"It has flashed through my mind," Richard admitted.

"Why has she refused you?"

Richard shook his head.

"Do you really think I qualify? If I cannot afford to buy a decent horse, I certainly cannot afford to keep an attractive women."

"Then why are you so interested in her?"

"As it happens, she had an introduction to me from Raymond Chatteris. You remember Raymond?"

"Yes, of course I do."

"When he was in trouble over a married woman, it was a question either of 'pistols at dawn' or of skipping the country, so he went to Paris in April."

"And met your friend Genevieve."

"Exactly!"

"He has obviously been very generous in paying back an old debt."

The Earl's voice was somethat mocking.

"I think, as it happens," Richard replied quite seriously, "he really wanted to do her a good turn, and he trusted me to guide her for the first month she is in England. I do not think I shall be wanted after that."

"You are beginning to intrigue me," the Earl said. "And by the way, Richard, what is her full name?"

14

"Just 'Genevieve.'"

The Earl looked puzzled and Richard explained:

"It is what she called herself in France, where, I understand, she had a small part in the Théâtre de Variétés. When she arrived in London and found how the Vestris calls herself 'Madam' and names all the cast on the programme as *Monsieur* this and *Mademoiselle* that, she decided to do the exact opposite and be just Genevieve. It is original, you must admit."

"I wonder who told her that would be a good thing to do," the Earl said mockingly.

They drove on, and Richard directed the Earl to a small Hotel situated at the back of the King's Theatre.

"She usually receives when she is having her hair done," Richard explained as the horses were drawn to a standstill. "I hope we are not too late. You will find her very attractive *en déshabillé*."

There was a cynical twist to the Earl's lips but he made no reply.

As he stepped into the small vestibule of the Hotel, he thought that Richard was diverting him far from what had been his intention when he had called on him this morning.

He was not for the moment interested in acquiring another mistress. His last one had been selected, he admitted now, rather hastily when he had first returned to London, and she had been a failure.

It was not the money he had expended on her that had irked him, but the fact that he considered he had wasted his time and shown, perhaps for the first time in his life, a lack of good taste.

Fay had, as it happened, been outstandingly lovely. It was only when he got to know her a little better that he had found that her inane conversation, and the way she giggled at everything or at nothing, got on his nerves, besides the fact that she was greedy almost to the point of absurdity.

15

It had been his own fault, he admitted, that he had ever become involved, and as Richard led him up the stairs to the first floor, he told himself that he would never again act in haste.

Richard knocked on a door which was opened somewhat theatrically by a maid attired in a mobcap trimmed with lace and an apron which matched it.

"*M'mselle* expec' you, *Monsieur*," she said in broken English, then saw with a look of surprise that Richard was not alone.

The Earl followed him into what was a quite decent-size room.

There was a bed draped with chiffon curtains in one corner of the room, and seated at a dressing-table in front of the bow-window which overlooked the street was a young woman trying on a fashionable bonnet.

Beside her stood a Milliner, with one bonnet in her hand and several others arrayed in their round boxes on the floor.

"*Monsieur* Rowlands, *M'mselle*," the maid announced from the door, "*et un autre gentilhomme.*"

The woman at the mirror turned round.

"Richard! *Quelle chance!* I need your advice. 'Ow do I look?"

There was no doubt of the answer she expected, for her small piquant face with flashing eyes fringed with dark eye-lashes and a red mouth that curved provocatively at the corners was framed by a black bonnet trimmed with lace, red ribbons, and scarlet roses.

Not only was the hat sensational, but Genevieve wore only a thin black nightgown which did little to conceal the perfection of her figure.

"Good-morning, Genevieve!" Richard said, raising her hand to his lips. "You must forgive me for arriving late, but I have brought with me someone I particularly want you to meet—the Earl of Hellington!"

He stood to one side as he spoke, and Genevieve held out her hand to the Earl.

"*Enchantée, Monsieur,*" she said. "Richard has told me much about you. I 'ope I not be disappointed."

The Earl, as was expected, kissed her hand.

"I hope so too, *Mademoiselle.*"

"*Asseyez-vous,*" Genevieve ordered, waving her hand in the direction of two chairs. "Richard, procure a drink *pour votre ami,* an' then both of you concentrate on me! I 'ave to buy *trois* or perhaps *quatre* bonnets and I need your advice. I need it *tout de suite!*"

As she spoke, she turned back to the mirror and stared at her reflection for a moment before she said:

"I not certain if in this I look *très jolie.* What you think?"

She looked into the mirror as she spoke, not at the gentlemen reflected in it, who had seated themselves on two rather uncomfortable chairs, the only ones in the room that were not cluttered with clothes or theatrical trophies of some sort or another, but at herself.

"Personally, *Mademoiselle,* I prefer you in the green one. It is not so dramatic, but it does not detract from your features as this one does."

The words were spoken in a soft, musical voice which was so different from Genevieve's and so unexpected from someone in her position that the Earl looked with curiosity at the speaker.

She was wearing a nondescript grey gown with a bonnet of the same colour and he thought he would not have noticed her if it had not been for her voice.

The sides of her bonnet made it difficult for him to see her face, and yet he had the impression of a small, straight nose, a firm chin, and a curved mouth whose soft pink colour owed nothing to artifice.

"*Peut-être vous avez raison,*" Genevieve said.

17

"Put on again, an' I ask *les gentilhommes* what they think."

The Milliner produced the green bonnet, and the moment it covered Genevieve's dark hair the Earl was aware how right the woman with the musical voice was.

As she said, it was far more becoming than the black and red one.

"You t'ink I am pretty, Milor? *Oui?*" Genevieve enquired.

"Very lovely!" the Earl agreed automatically.

As he spoke, he was waiting to hear the Milliner speak again.

"Then I take this one," Genevieve said, "and ze other two we 'ave already chosen. Put 'em on ze bed."

The Milliner took the three bonnets and moved across the room to place them on the bed, which had a frilled cover decorated with large bows of velvet ribbon.

The Earl, watching her, thought she moved with a grace that he might have expected from an actress rather than a saleswoman.

It was still impossible to see her face because of the way the sides of her bonnet obscured it, but he was sure that she had not looked directly at him.

She walked back again to the dressing-table to begin tying up the boxes in which the bonnets had been packed.

"You 'ave ze bill?" Genevieve asked.

"Yes, *Mademoiselle*."

"*Vous savez* what to do wi 'it. *Les Anglais pas differents* from ze way they are *en Paris*."

It was obvious that the milliner did not undererstand, and in an amused voice the Earl said mockingly:

"What *Mademoiselle* means is that the spectators must always pay for the entertainment. Bring the bill to me."

For the first time the Milliner looked up at him and he saw the astonishment in her eyes. Then Genevieve gave a little laugh.

"*Tiens, Monsieur, vous êtes très gentil!* It is not what I mean, *mais je suis très* . . . grateful. 'Ow shall I thank you?"

She sprang from the stool on which she was sitting and, moving towards the Earl, bent and kissed his cheek.

As she did so, he was conscious of the exotic perfume Genevieve used, and for the moment the warmth of her barely covered body pressed against him.

Then she was moving towards Richard, saying:

"'Ave you forgotten, *mon cher* Richard, that I also am thirsty?"

"No, of course not," Richard replied, "and I have a drink ready for you."

"*Merci, mon cher.*"

He knew that she thanked him not only for the drink but for introducing her to the Earl.

He smiled at her in a slightly conspiratorial manner, studiously ignoring the fact that the Earl was counting out quite a number of guineas from his purse.

The Earl had not taken the bill, which was neatly written in a flowing hand, from the saleswoman but had left her holding it.

She stood very straight and still beside him, and, looking up, he could see her face clearly. He thought she was not only very different from what he had thought a saleswoman would look like but also unexpectedly lovely.

It was not only her large eyes in her small oval face that surprised him, it was her clear-cut features, which had an almost classical look about them.

"Do you make these bonnets yourself?" he asked.

"Some of them, My Lord."

"You must be very skilful."

19

She did not reply but merely acknowledged his compliment with a little inclination of her head.

"Do you enjoy your work?"

Again there was no answer, and with another nod of her head signified the affirmative.

The Earl had the feeling that she was being deliberately aloof, and he was certain that she resented the fact that he was speaking to her, as if it was an intrusion on her privacy.

Because he was determined to hear her voice again, he said:

"I asked you a question."

"I ... work as a necessity ... My Lord."

Her voice was still musical but there was a note in it which told him that she would have liked to tell him to mind his own business.

He now had the right amount of guineas in his hand, but he did not give them to her.

"It must be somewhat frustrating," he said, "to spend one's life adorning other women so that they should look beautiful."

Just for a moment the corners of her mouth twitched and he thought he saw the suspicion of a twinkle in her downcast eyes, if she told him without words that for many women, whatever one did to make them look beautiful and however much they hoped and paid, it was an impossible task.

It was strange, the Earl thought, but he knew that was what she was thinking, even though she had said not a word.

The Milliner stood waiting, and now as if she felt that he was being unnecessarily tardy in paying the bill, she held out her hand.

It was a small, exquisitely shaped hand with long thin fingers, and the Earl noted she wore no rings.

"Thank you, My Lord."

She was prompting him, almost demanding the

money, and, as if she goaded him into a reply, he said:

"Here is the amount which is on the bill, and here is a guinea for yourself."

It was then that she raised her eyes to look into his and he saw a flash of anger in them.

For one moment he thought she was about to refuse to accept his "tip." Then, almost as if she recollected something, perhaps the position in which she found herself, she merely said in what he thought was a deliberately meek manner:

"Thank you . . . My Lord. I am . . . of course . . . grateful."

She curtseyed, took the money from his hand, and turned away with what was suspiciously like a little flounce of her gown.

Then she gathered up her boxes and left the room without speaking another word, not even to her client.

Chapter Two

Thalia came out through the back door of Mrs. Burton's Millinery Shop and looked to where at the end of the street a figure was waiting.

She hurried towards an elderly woman dressed like a respectable servant, who smiled as she approached.

"I am sorry, Hannah, if I kept you waiting," Thalia said, "but there were a lot of boxes to pack up at the last moment. Thank goodness I did not have to deliver them."

"It's not right for you to do such menial jobs anyway!" Hannah answered crossly.

Thalia laughed.

"Beggars cannot be choosers, as you well know, and actually I have had a most entertaining day. I will not tell you about it now but will wait until we reach Mama. How is she?"

"As she always is," Hannah replied, "counting the days until your father's return and watching for a letter that never comes!"

Again Hannah's voice was sharp with anger, and Thalia understood, because if there was one person whom Hannah adored it was her mother.

They walked briskly along the streets, which were not so crowded as they had been earlier in the day, until they reached Hay Hill.

At the bottom, they crossed the road and entered Lansdowne Passage.

As often as Thalia walked along the passage which lay between the garden of Lansdowne House and that of Devonshire House, she invariably found herself thinking of Highwaymen.

The Prince of Wales and the Duke of York, when they were very young men, were once driving in a hackney-carriage down Hay Hill when they were stopped and robbed by a group of Highwaymen.

Those thieves were never caught, and another time a Highwayman escaping from Piccadilly rode down Lansdowne Passage, put his horse to the steps at the Curzon Street end, and galloped away.

It always seemed to Thalia a reckless and exciting escapade and she invariably found herself wondering if, had she been in the same position, she would have been so clever.

Hannah disliked talking when they were hurrying home and Thalia therefore continued with her own thoughts without interruption.

The gentleman who had given her the guinea in *Mademoiselle* Genevieve's room this morning had the look, she thought, of a Highwayman or perhaps a buccaneer.

He was exactly the type of man she liked to watch either riding in the Row or walking down Bond Street.

She had not until now had the chance of speaking with what she imagined was one of the *Beaux*, and his cynical, rather mocking voice was just the way she had anticipated he would speak.

Now that they were in Curzon Street, Hannah seemed to move even more quickly, and a few minutes later they had turned left under an archway which led them into Shepherd's Market.

Here again Thalia's imagination made her people the place with the Fair which she had read about in books and which had been described to her by many of the older inhabitants of the Market.

Shepherd's Market was still a little village with its own independent life, but in the past the Fair which had been held there for two weeks every year had been one of the sights of London.

It had started as an annual Market, but in the surrounding fields and streets there had been booths for jugglers, prize-fighters, wild beasts, and mountebanks.

A merry-go-round, swings, fire-eaters, and rope-dancers had drawn the gaping crowds which had found the pig-faced women, the monstrosities, and the cannibal chiefs an irresistible entertainment.

But it had not always been fun, Thalia remembered. There had been tragedies too.

Over a hundred years ago there had been a tight-rope dancer known as "Lady Mary" who was said to be the daughter of a foreign nobleman.

She had eloped with a showman who taught her how to dance on a tight-rope, and her performance was immensely popular as she had both grace and skill.

She had continued with her act after she became pregnant and one day she over-balanced and fell. She gave birth to a still-born child and died almost at once.

Thalia often thought of Lady Mary because although it was a sad story, it was a very romantic one.

She must, she thought, have loved her husband very deeply to have left her luxurious home in Florence for such a strange way of life.

But now at one of the small houses at the far end of Shepherd's Market, Hannah had stopped and drawn a large key from a pocket in her sensible-looking black skirt.

She opened the door and Thalia ran past her to call as she hurried up the narrow staircase:

"Mama, I am back!"

She opened a door and entered what would have been called a Drawing-Room if such a tiny building could boast of anything so pretentious.

It was now converted into a bedroom, and lying on a chaise-longue in front of the window was a woman who still retained her beauty although she looked frail and ill.

She held out both hands to her daughter and Thalia ran across the room to kiss her on both cheeks.

"I am back, Mama, and I have so much to tell you. Have you been very dull here all day?"

"I have been all right, my dearest," her mother replied softly. "But I admit to waiting impatiently for your return. You seem to bring the sunshine with you."

"That is what I would like to bring," Thalia said, "but instead I have brought you something which will make you laugh and will purchase food, which at the moment is more important than the sunshine."

As she spoke, she drew the guinea from her purse and held it up for her mother to see.

"My first 'tip,'" she said, "and from a Gentleman of Fashion."

Her mother gave a little gasp.

"You cannot mean, Thalia, that you actually accepted money from a man?"

Thalia laughed.

She was taking off her concealing bonnet and now she flung it down on a chair and patted her golden hair, which had tiny red lights in it, into place.

"I admit, Mama, I felt like throwing it at him, but then I remembered that I am a humble Milliner."

Her mother gave a little groan.

"Oh, Thalia, how can I bear to think of you working in such conditions and being treated as if you were nothing more than a servant?"

"That is exactly what I am," Thalia said. "But,

Mama, it was such fun today! If you only saw the women who came in to buy bonnets!"

She gave a little laugh at the remembrance of them, and went on:

"One looked exactly like a cottage-loaf and her face was as big as a pumpkin. She kept saying to me: 'Do you really think I look pretty in this?' I longed to tell her she could not look pretty in anything."

"I hope you did nothing of the sort!" her mother said reprovingly. "That would be unkind."

"No, of course not, Mama. I told her she looked charming and persuaded her to buy three bonnets instead of two. Mrs. Burton was delighted with me."

She sat down on a chair beside her mother and took her hand in hers.

"Do not be shocked about the guinea, dearest," she said. "It will buy you some delicious things to eat, a chicken, lots of eggs, cream, and many more luxuries which the Doctor ordered."

Her mother did not reply and Thalia knew that nothing the Doctor could prescribe could heal an anxious heart that was growing near to despair.

As she looked at the sadness in her mother's face, Thalia asked herself why her father, wherever he was, had not written.

She had sent dozens of letters to the address he had given them in America, but after the first six months he had been away, there had been no more news of him.

It was terrible to see her mother suffering so acutely, growing paler and thinner every day, and to know that there was nothing she could do about it.

The three years of her father's exile were nearly at an end and she was sure that if he was alive he would come home.

He could not be so cruel as to stay away when he knew how desperately they needed him.

As if she wished to divert her mother's mind from where it always lingered with her father, Thalia told her in detail about her visit to *Mademoiselle* Genevieve at the Hotel near the King's Theater and how, having chosen three bonnets, she had made the Earl of Hellington pay for them.

She told the story amusingly, omitting the facts that the ballet-dancer wore only her nightgown and that she had kissed the Earl in gratitude.

As it was, her mother was shocked at the Frenchwoman's behavior.

"How can I bear to think of you, my dearest, associating with such women?"

"I have heard Papa talking about 'bits o' muslin,'" Thalia said, "but I never expected to speak to any of them. She was extremely attractive, Mama, and I am sure she dances beautifully."

"Dearest, you must find something else to do."

The laughter died out of Thalia's eyes.

"Mama, you know as well as I do that I am very lucky to have employment of any sort, and it was actually you who thought I should be a Milliner."

"I did?"

"Yes, Mama. When I was trimming that old bonnet of mine you said: 'You are so skilful with your fingers, dearest child, I do not believe that even Bond Street could produce anything more stylish than you have just contrived out of those old ribbons and the silk flowers I bought over five years ago.'"

"I did not mean you to sell your skill," her mother said, "even while I admit it is unusual."

"We had nothing else left to sell," Thalia replied simply, "and even Hannah disliked the idea of starving to death."

Her mother said no more.

She was thinking that when her husband had to flee the country, he had thought that with what he had left them they would at least be comfortably provided for until his return.

It had been one of those dramatic and unexpected events that had dropped like a meteor from the skies to change the lives of people when they were least expecting it.

Sir Denzil Caversham had always been a charming but impetuous man who, ever since he was a small boy, had got into unexpected scrapes.

He had been in trouble at School, at his University, and even at one time in his Regiment.

Then he had married and settled down and his relatives had thought their anxieties regarding him were over.

He would live the quiet life of the country squire, happy with his beautiful wife and content with the ancient Manor House and Estate which had been in the Caversham family for five hundred years.

But Sir Denzil was a man who needed friends and he had found it impossible to keep away from his Clubs and from the excitement and entertainments of London, where the companions of his more raffish days welcomed his return effusively.

Although he could not afford it, he and his wife had rented a house in Mayfair for the Season, and regardless of expenses had entertained until they were back in the swim of what was known as the *Beau Monde*.

As Lady Caversham was extremely beautiful, she had enjoyed the Balls, the Receptions, and the Assemblies almost as much as her husband had.

They returned to the country only for the hunting and shooting and gradually had begun to spend more time in London, arriving almost before the daffodils were in bud and leaving long after the Season had come to an end, with the Regent moving from Carlton House to Brighton.

It was only Thalia who missed the country, even though she enjoyed the teachers and tutors who came to the house in Brook Street.

But they could not make up for the fact that

riding in Hyde Park was not the same as riding over the fields at home, and her dogs had to be left behind because in London she could not exercise them as much as they needed.

Then three years ago disaster had struck.

Sir Denzil, who was inclined to be unpredictable especially when he had been drinking, got into an argument at White's Club over some quite trivial subject that ended in his being insulted.

Thalia was never quite certain what was the real source of the quarrel in the first place, although she suspected it concerned a woman.

Whatever it was, it resulted in Sir Denzil being involved in a duel; his opponent was a Statesman of considerable importance.

They met at dawn in St. James's Park and Lady Caversham was not told what was happening until the duel was over.

Not that she could have done anything to prevent it, because a challenge, once given and accepted, involved the honour of the participants and there was no going back.

The first thing Thalia knew about it was when she went into her mother's room to bid her good-morning and Lady Caversham said:

"I cannot imagine what has happened, Thalia. When I woke, your father was not here. It is not like him to leave the house without telling me where he is going. It is too early for him to be riding."

Neither of them could imagine what had occurred, until half-an-hour later they heard footsteps coming up the stairs.

"Here is Papa!" Thalia said. "Now he will be able to tell you, Mama, where he has been."

Sir Denzil entered the bedroom and his wife gave a little cry.

"What has—happened? Why do you—look like that?"

"I have killed him!" Sir Denzil said.

"Killed—who?" Lady Caversham cried.

"Spencer Talbot," he answered. "And now I have to leave the country."

"Leave the—country?"

Lady Caversham could barely whisper the words.

"I have already seen the Lord Chancellor," Sir Denzil explained. "It was the only thing I could do in the circumstances. After all, Talbot was in the Cabinet, and the first thing I realised was that there must be no scandal which would affect the Government."

"How could you kill him? How is it possible?"

"I meant only to wing him in the arm," Sir Denzil said, "but he moved at the last moment, I think because he intended from the very first to kill me. His temper is proverbial."

"Instead . . . you killed . . . him!"

Thalia heard her own voice say the words and was surprised that she had spoken.

"Yes, I have killed him," Sir Denzil said, "and because Lord Eldon is insistent that there should be no scandal, the whole thing will be hushed up and it will be announced that Talbot has died of a heart-attack. But I am to go abroad for three years."

"Three—years!" Lady Caversham echoed faintly.

"It might have been five, or even life," Sir Denzil said, "but, knowing Talbot's temper, the Lord Chancellor has been lenient to me, as he pointed out in no uncertain terms."

"But three—years, dearest! Where will you go?"

"Anywhere in Europe is impossible, I realise that," Sir Denzil replied, "and I have no wish to be a prisoner of Bonaparte. No, I shall go to America."

"To . . . America!"

Thalia's voice echoed round the room, because she was so astonished.

America seemed far away, a land of unpredictable people who had thrown out the British, a land full, she thought, of red Indians and black people who had been brought there from Africa to work as slaves.

After that, there had been a wild commotion of packing what her father needed and getting him off to Plymouth, where, he had already learnt, there was a ship preparing to sail across the Atlantic.

His wife wanted to go with him but he would not hear of it.

"God knows what sort of discomforts I shall have to endure," Sir Denzil had said. "It will be hard enough, my darling, without having to worry about you. Yet three years will pass quickly and I will soon be with you again."

It all sounded a sensible idea, despite her mother's misery at being parted from the man she loved.

As soon as it was learnt, and it was impossible to pretend otherwise, that Sir Denzil had left the country, the bills came pouring in.

Because her mother was so unhappy, Thalia, although she was only fifteen, had tried to help the family Solicitor, whom she had known ever since she was a child, to sort things out.

Thalia was never certain how the rumour began, but the story got about that Sir Denzil had been exiled for life and could never return to England.

It was difficult to explain the true facts, and, as in all rumours, there was no single person they could actually discover who had started the story in the first place.

The tradesmen grew more and more pressing, and in the end the only thing they could do was to shut up the Manor House and move to London, renting a house in Shepherd's Market for a few pounds a month.

There, they lived on the sale of Lady Caversham's jewels, which were her own property.

Everything that belonged to Sir Denzil was either sold or mortgaged, the Manor House and its contents fortunately being entailed onto his heirs.

At first Thalia thought that if they lived frugally without any extravagances, they could manage to exist until her father returned.

Then, when the letters from him ceased and they had no news, her mother grew ill. There were Doctor's bills and soon their little store of money disappeared.

Owing to the war, luxury foods were more expensive, and when it became a case of their actually being hungry, Thalia knew she had to do something.

She had in fact for the last year been planning a way in which she thought she could augment their income, but that was a secret she kept even from her mother and it was unfortunately something that was not likely to show a return very quickly.

Therefore, she told herself that she must get employment of some sort, and it was her mother who had given her the idea of trimming bonnets.

Since the war had ended the previous year, clothes had become more elaborate and bonnets were at times almost garishly decorated to match the gowns which were trimmed with lace and ruchings, embroidery and bows.

Mrs. Burton, to whom she had gone first, had said that she had no vacancy in her shop and certainly not for somebody without previous experience.

Then she had been astute enough to realise that Thalia's beauty, the educated manner in which she spoke, and her whole appearance might be an asset.

She had looked her up and down very critically and found it difficult to find fault.

"I will give you a trial in the work-room," she had said at length. "But if you are not satisfactory, you can leave without notice and without making any fuss."

"I accept your conditions, Madam," Thalia had replied.

Mrs. Burton had offered a remuneration for her services which was so small as to be almost ludicrous, but Thalia did not complain.

She told herself that once she was in the position, she would make herself indispensable and her finances would improve.

Mrs. Burton, although she was not prepared to say so, had been astounded not only by the artistry with which Thalia could trim bonnets but, when she was promoted to the front of the shop, by the skill with which she would flatter a customer into buying more than she had at first intended.

"I could not do better myself,' she often thought.

But she had no intention of saying so, knowing that if a shop-woman was praised she invariably expected her wages to escalate accordingly.

In April, when Mrs. Burton's shop was run off its feet in preparation for the Royal Wedding of Princess Charlotte of England and Prince Leopold of Belgium, which was to take place on May 4, Thalia became, as she had intended, indispensable.

Although her mother was still horrified that she must deman herself to work in a shop, she and Hannah were glad of the money that she brought home.

Now, as if she had been thinking over what Thalia had been saying to her, Lady Caversham asked:

"Is it really necessary, dearest, for you to come in contact with gentlemen like the Earl of Hellington? I do not remember your father speaking of him, but if he does not treat you as a lady, it will be because of the invidious position in which you are placed."

"I told you, Mama,' he treated me as if I was a Milliner," Thalia said with laughter in her voice, "and tipped me for my pains."

Lady Caversham shuddered.

"I cannot bear to think of it," she said.

Then with a little cry she exclaimed:

"He did not know who you were?"

"No, of course not, Mama," Thalia answered, "and even if he had asked my name, Mrs. Burton, as you are well aware, knows me only as 'Miss Carver.'"

Lady Caversham sighed.

"Such a common name!" she had protested when Thalia had told her it was the name she had chosen.

"That is what it is intended to be," Thalia had replied. "'Carver' is good old English and doubtless it derives from the butchers who carve the meat."

She had chosen it deliberately because it was as near as possible to "Caversham," knowing how hard it would be, if she was asked quickly, to remember not to give her real name.

Her mother had been as horrified by the subterfuge as she was by everything else which Thalia's working entailed.

But Lady Caversham had, in her ignorance, thought that being in a ladies' shop was at least some protection from the gentlemen who wandered up and down Bond Street looking for attractive women who frequented that street.

Mrs. Burton did not sell only bonnets, although since Thalia's arrival they had become her most important item of sale.

The Milliners furnished to ladies everything that could contribute to or set off their beauty and, as some writer had said, "increase their vanity or render them ridiculous."

Lady Caversham had no idea, nor had Thalia until she worked in a shop, how many gentlemen escorted the lady of their fancy when she went shopping, or how many were expected to pay for what was purchased.

Mrs. Burton soon realised that Thalia was too attractive to serve the Social Ladies who were accompanied by their rich lovers and therefore she always waited on them herself.

Thalia was at her best with women who were so plain and unattractive that it was doubtful if any man would look at them with or without an alluring bonnet.

The gentlemen would lounge in chairs on the other side of the room while some fashionable beauty stared at her reflection in the mirror until the moment when she asked his approval, pouting her red lips as she did so.

"They make me sick," Thalia had said to herself. "If I were a man, I would be put off by all those stupid affectations."

She came to the conclusion, however, that a great number of the gentlemen she saw in Mrs. Burton's shop were as empty-headed as the women they escorted, and she noted critically the behaviour of both sexes.

Now, because she did not wish to go on talking about anything that might prove distressing or upsetting, she said to Lady Caversham:

"I am going to change, dearest, and then when we have had supper, I am going to read to you from a book of Lord Byron's poetry which has just been published."

She saw Lady Caversham's eyes light up and she explained:

"On the way back from *Mademoiselle* Genevieve's this morning I stopped at Hatchard's in Piccadilly and bought the book. I know you will enjoy it, Mama."

"I am sure of it, dearest. But surely that was rather extravagant?"

"We can afford it," Thalia replied.

She was about to add that she had been feeling especially rich because she had the Earl's guinea in her purse, although the circumstances in which she had received it made her feel as if it burned a hole in her pocket.

But she had wanted to give her mother a treat and she had also had another reason for going to Hatchard's.

Now she bent down and kissed Lady Caversham, saying:

"Stop worrying, Mama. It will not be long before Papa is home, and you know as well as I do that with the storms we have had this winter, half the ships carrying mail to England from the other side of the world never reached their destination."

"Supposing—he never comes—home?" Lady Caversham said in a very low voice.

"He will, I know he will," Thalia said. "I 'feel it in my bones,' as Hannah says, and you know you told me once, Mama, that because you and Papa were so close, if he had died you would have been aware of it."

"I suppose that is true," Lady Caversham agreed.

"Of course it is true," Thalia said. "You have to believe in Papa and trust him. He is alive, and if he comes home and sees you looking as pale as you are now, he will be furious with me and will never believe that I have done my best to look after you."

"Oh, my dearest, you have done everything anyone could do, and a great deal more besides," Lady Caversham said. "It is just that I pray and pray that I shall hear from him, but somehow my prayers do not seem to be heard. If only I could have a letter."

"You do not want a letter," Thalia said firmly, "you want Papa! One day he will walk in when you least expect it."

"Suppose he cannot find us?"

"Now, Mama, we have talked about this over and over again," Thalia said. "Everyone in the country will be ready to tell him. Mr. Johnson, who runs the Green Man, and old Hibbert, who is looking after the house, are waiting for him to appear."

She paused, then added:

"I also went to our house in Brook Street the

other day. As it is empty again, I left a piece of paper stuck on the door saying that all enquiries regarding Lady Caversham should be made to this address."

"You think of everything, dearest."

"I try to," Thalia said, "but you have to help me, Mama, by getting well and a great deal fatter than you are at the moment."

Lady Caversham smiled.

"If I do that," she said, "I shall have to ask you to let out my gowns, and you know you have no time at the moment."

"When you talk like that, Mama, I feel we are back in the old days with you and Papa, making a joke of everything and the whole house seeming to be filled with sunshine."

She saw the longing in her mother's eyes and added quickly:

"And that is what it will be, mark my words, by the end of the summer. Papa will be with us and we shall all be laughing at something absurd he has done."

Her mother was smiling as Thalia went to her own room on the other side of the landing. It was barely larger than a cupboard.

They had been lucky to find such a cheap house and she knew it was because the kind of artisans who lived with their families in Shepherd's Market usually had a number of children, so small a house could not have accommodated them.

Downstairs was the kitchen, where Hannah reigned supreme, and a very small Sitting-Room facing the street.

It was here that Thalia kept her papers, and before she went into the kitchen where Hannah had prepared her mother's supper that she would carry upstairs, she made a few notes.

As she put her quill-pen back into its holder she looked longingly at what she had written, as if she would have liked to go on writing.

Then resolutely she went from the small room, shutting the door behind her.

* * *

The Earl walked into White's Club to cause a sensation by his sudden reappearance.

"Good God, Hellington!" someone exclaimed. "We thought you had gone rustic and we had lost you! Do you realise you have been away for three weeks?"

"I am aware of it," the Earl replied, seating himself amongst the Club's select "inner circle" as a matter of right.

They were all close friends, including the Duke of Argyll, Lord Alvanley, Lord Worcester, "Poodle" Byng, and Sir Lumley Skeffington.

They sat in the bow-window which had been sacred to Beau Brummell. It was there that he had reigned supreme and his pronouncements were listened to as if he had the wisdom of Solomon.

Not only the Earl but a great number of other Members thought White's had never been the same since Brummell's debts had caught up with him and he had been forced to make a quick escape across the Channel to where he was now living in a Lodging-House in Calais.

"What was the country like?" someone asked, as if it were a foreign land.

"Hot!" the Earl replied.

Because he had no desire to talk about himself, he asked:

"What were you laughing about when I arrived? I could hear you from the pavement."

"Alvanley was reading from a new book that has just been published," replied "Poodle" Byng.

"A book?" the Earl enquired.

It seemed an unlikeley subject for his friends at White's, but Lord Alvanley, who was noted as a wit, held up a small volume.

The Earl read what was written on the cover:

GENTLEMEN

by a
Person of Quality

"You find it amusing?" he asked.
"Just listen," Lord Alvanley replied.
He turned several pages before he said:
"Here is one the others have not heard:

*"In the race for a Gentleman's affections, his
horses come first, his Club second, his dogs third.
Also ran are a number of pretty women, but they
seldom last the course."*

Those listening laughed and the Earl said:
"It certainly sounds amusing."
"Give us another!" Lord Worcester begged.
Lord Alvanley turned a page and read:

*"A Gentleman does not listen at key-holes, but
then he listens to no-one but himself!"*

"That is you, 'Poodle'!" the Duke of Argyll said.
"The 'Person of Quality' must have met you!"
"Here is another!" Lord Alvanley said.

*"A Gentleman is too sporting to pull his horses
or cheat at cards, but he has no qualms about
seducing his best friend's wife!"*

The Earl looked round his circle of friends.
"Which of you is responsible for this?" he asked.
"I doubt if it is you, Skeffington, but I rather suspect
Alvanley."
"I swear to you on my honour that I have not
written it, even though I would like to have done so,"
Lord Alvanley replied. "But now that I think of it, it

is too witty to have been written by anyone who is not a Member."

"Sheer conceit!" the Earl snapped. "A great number of the Members of this Club are incapable of writing their own names, let alone a book!"

They laughed and teased one another, but while he was talking Lord Alvanley had put the book down on the table in front of him and the Earl picked it up.

There were not many pages but on each one there were six witty comments, and yet there was nothing vicious in what was said. The Earl read:

A Gentleman has two sets of rules regarding infidelity, one for himself and another for his wife.

Below this was:

A Dandy is like a peacock: all tail and little brain.

He thought that applied to all the Dandies he knew, whom he despised. Aloud he said:

"I wonder if we shall ever discover who the author is. I think he will be far too discreet to admit that he is responsible for what a number of people would find uncomfortably true."

"You speak for yourself, Hellington!" the Duke of Argyll answered. "I refuse to admit that anything the book says is the truth, and, what is more, I resent the impertinence of somebody we might even call a friend putting us in print."

"I agree with you," Lord Worcester said, "it is unsporting."

"If you ask me," the Earl said, "you all have guilty consciences and are frightened of what you will read next. But at least, as far as I can ascertain, the author mentions no names."

"That is one good thing, at any rate," Lord Worcester said. "At the same time, I shall try to discover who is the traitor in our midst, and when we know, we will make it extremely uncomfortable for him to remain in the Club."

"Personally, I could not care what he writes," the Earl said, "and in the case of the innuendoes, if the cap fits, then one must be prepared to wear it."

"That is very high-handed, Vargus," said Richard, who had remained silent up until now. "You are only able to feel so 'cock-a-hoop' because you are quite certain there is no scandal written about you, but a lot of people are in a very different position."

There was silence after he had spoken. Then Lord Worcester said hastily:

"That is true enough. People have no right to go snooping round and writing about their friends and acquaintances, then being too cowardly to give their name. I vote that we find out who it is and have him 'black-balled.'"

The Earl laughed.

"You are all making a mountain out of a molehill. As far as I can see, there is nothing slanderous in anything that is written here; they are just generally amusing quips about gentlemen in general."

"If the newspapers get hold of it they will make us look pretty ridiculous!" the Duke of Argyll said harshly.

"Personally, I do not care what they say," the Earl replied. "It is only women who read the gossip anyway."

The Earl spoke in the lofty tone which always made Richard smile.

He was well aware that the Earl never gossiped and was never interested even in the juiciest scandals.

The majority of the Members of White's were quite prepared to talk about one another, and a number of them were always ready to whisper in a corner about what had happened the night before and reveal which husbands were being cuckolded by their closest friends.

He was not surprised when a little later on the Earl rose restlessly and left the Club.

He did not invite Richard to join him and he watched him wistfully from the bow-window as he drove off in his Phaeton up St. James's Street.

He wondered where he was going and wished he had asked.

Last night had been more amusing than he had anticipated. At the first Ball they had attended, he and the Earl had found friends there who had been delighted to see them and they had sat drinking in the card-room and had made no effort to join the dancers.

At Ashburnham House, the Princess had held out her arms in greeting and scolded the Earl for being away for so long.

"London has been dull without you," she had said, "but now that you are back, My Lord, we must celebrate."

She had introduced him to a number of beautiful women, none of whom Richard thought would be of any use to the Earl in his search for a wife.

At least two of them had intimated before the evening was over that they would be willing to play a very different role in his life when their husbands were otherwise engaged.

Another tried determinedly to enlist his help in promoting a young man with whom she declared herself hopelessly and crazily in love.

"Altogether it was an enjoyable evening," Richard had told himself when he got back to his lodgings, "but it was extremely unfruitful from Vargus's point of view."

He needed a vast amount of self-control to prevent himself from asking the Earl if he intended to further his acquaintance with Genevieve.

He knew that if there was one thing his friend really disliked, it was being cross-questioned about the women in his life.

Richard himself admired Genevieve so much that he could not believe the Earl would be any less enthusiastic than he was and would not take the opportunity of capturing her before he found he had other rivals.

At the same time, the Earl was always unpredictable and Richard would have thought him even more so if he had known where he was going at this moment.

* * *

The Earl drove his Phaeton to Bond Street, and when he was some doors away from where he knew Mrs. Burton had her shop, he drew his horses to a standstill.

"Walk them, Henry," he said to his groom, then proceeded to walk leisurely down the street.

Thinking over his encounter yesterday with the French ballet-dancer, he had come to the conclusion that he was more interested in the little Milliner.

He found himself remembering not only the musical quality of her voice but also the flash of anger that had appeared in her eyes when he had tipped her.

It was certainly unexpected, and that it had happened intrigued him.

He also remembered the faint suspicion of dimples and the twinkle in her down-cast eyes when something amused her.

He might be mistaken, he might easily be disappointed, but he had the feeling that he would like to see her again. However, for the moment he was not quite certain how to go about it.

He knew where she worked because Mrs. Burton's name was inscribed on the bonnet-boxes which she had carried from the room when she left without bidding anyone good-bye.

The Earl was sure that the reason why her departure had been so precipitate was the fact that he had given her a guinea.

He had expended a great many more guineas on Genevieve, and when he and Richard had left and she had thanked him even more profusely the second time, he had found her methods too obvious to be intriguing.

What was more, the blatant way she displayed her body robbed her of the mystery which the Earl liked to find in the women he fancied.

It continually irked him that when he was with ladies of the *Beau Monde* or the "Fashionable Impures," they never allowed him to do his own hunting.

Almost before he made up his mind that he was interested in them, they were making it unmistakably obvious that they were very interested in him.

Last night he had known that it was only a matter of time and opportunity before he could, if he wished, go to bed with both the women to whom the Princess had introduced him, and accordingly he found himself retreating rather than advancing.

He spent more time thinking of the troubles of the woman in love than of the considerable attractions of the other two.

He had known that she was sincere and he had liked the manner in which she spoke naturally and unpretentiously in order to plead the cause of the man she loved.

The Earl had long ago admitted to himself that one thing he hoped to find in a woman was a certain unpredictability.

It was like playing a game of chess with an experienced opponent whose moves were never expected and were therefore exciting and stimulating.

Unfortunately, the women he met up with were

predictable to the point where he could anticipate every move they made and every word they said.

It was this which made him afraid of marriage.

How could he endure the boredom of knowing what remark his wife would make before she made it, of knowing there were no surprises in store for him tomorrow, the day after, or the day after that?

There was one thing about horses, he told himself often enough—that even the best trained and the most reliable could sometimes surprise, disconcert, and even infuriate one.

When he thought of horses he remembered the phrase which Lord Alvanley had read aloud, and he told himself that it was unmistakably true that in a race for his affections, his horses came in first.

Nevertheless, he decided he would have a look at the little Milliner again.

He would doubtless be disillusioned, but at least it would be amusing, if nothing else, to make her eyes flash with anger, then watch her force herself to be humbly subservient.

Mrs. Burton's shop was the next in the street and he would reach it within a few footsteps.

He stopped almost as if he were reconnoitring his position as he had often done in France.

Even as he stared into a shop-window which, although he was unaware of it, was a Pharmacist's, he heard a voice cry from a carriage:

"Vargus! Is it really you?"

There was no mistaking who spoke, and as the Earl took his hat from his head he thought it was unfortunate that he had encountered Lady Adelaide so soon after returning to London.

He had in fact been relieved that she had not been at either of the Balls last night, knowing that she would have clung to him in that possessive manner that he found extremely irritating.

"You are back, Vargus!" she said.

45

She alighted from her carriage and was standing beside him and looking up at him with an unmistakable enticement in her slanting dark eyes.

"As you see, I am back," the Earl replied.

"Why did you not tell me?"

"I only returned yesterday."

"You knew I would be waiting breathlessly for your return! Surely Richard must have told you how perturbed I was at your long absence in the country?"

She paused and looked at him suspiciously.

"If it was the country which kept you?"

"If there is one thing I find tiresome, it is being expected to make explanations about what I have done or have not done," the Earl replied sharply.

Then an idea came to him. In a very different voice he said:

"To make reparation for my misdeeds, I will give you a new bonnet. Why do we not repair to Mrs. Burton's shop and see what she has that will suit you?"

"Vargus!"

For a moment Lady Adelaide's breath was taken away.

Never until now had the Earl offered her presents of any sort, with the exception of flowers which she knew were ordered for him by his secretary as a matter of form.

"A bonnet!" she went on. "But of course, I would love one!"

It struck her that a bonnet was a rather intimate present, something a man might give to a woman to whom he was attracted but not if his intentions were serious.

Then she told herself quickly that she was not a young girl to be compromised by a present, whatever it might be, and that the Earl should give her anything was certainly a step in the right direction.

"I can imagine," she said, "no better way to celebrate your home-coming, and, as you say, Mrs. Burton's is next door."

"Let us go there," the Earl said. "I have a feeling, Adelaide, that no woman has enough bonnets in her life."

"Of course not, nor enough *Beaux*," Lady Adelaide replied with what was meant to be a glance of admiration.

She did not realise that the Earl's lips tightened for a moment at the word and that he had a strong desire to tell her that he had changed his mind.

Then, Lady Adelaide chattering gaily, they walked into Mrs. Burton's shop, and the Earl, as he had expected, saw a slight figure in a grey gown, waiting on a customer.

Chapter Three

The Earl, driving his Phaeton down a somewhat scruffy street into which he knew the back-doors of the Bond Street shops opened, thought he had been very clever.

One glance at the little Milliner whom he had seen the day before had told him she was even more alluring than he remembered, and her hair, particularly, was a colour that was unique.

He realised that it was a hue chorus-girls attempted to attain with the use of dye-pots, only to be disappointed.

There was no doubt that in the Milliner's case it was natural and a perfect frame for her large eyes.

She was very thin, which gave her a spiritual grace that made Lady Adelaide look heavy and somewhat clumsy.

The Earl was far too shrewd to stare too obviously across the shop or to appear to be interested in anything except the lady he was accompanying.

Lady Adelaide was in her element.

She was so elated at the thought of the Earl giving her a present and seeming to be more effusive than usual that she chattered away, flirting with him with side-long glances and an invitation on her red lips which she felt he must find irresistible.

Mrs. Burton produced a number of extremely attractive bonnets for Lady Adelaide to try on.

Each time she turned to ask the Earl's opinion she was sure that there was a look of admiration in his eyes, and as she was determined to spin out for as long as possible the time they were together, she kept on asking to see yet another creation.

She must have tried on nearly a dozen when the Earl said to Mrs. Burton:

"I saw a bonnet I rather admired yesterday. One of your assistants was showing it to a client at Fletcher's Hotel near Drury Lane."

Lady Adelaide was still.

She was immediately curious as to who the Earl was visiting in that vicinity and suspected it was a performer either at the King's Theatre or at Covent Garden.

In the circumstances, the woman was not likely to trouble her particularly. But she had no wish for him to take another mistress, having learnt from Richard that his interest in one whom he had recently housed and provided with some quite outstanding jewellery was now at an end.

If he was going to be generous with jewels in the future, Lady Adelaide was determined to have them herself, although what she really craved was nothing more expensive than a gold wedding-ring.

She was, however, wise enough not to interrupt but to listen to what was said as Mrs. Burton replied to the Earl:

"Can Your Lordship describe the bonnet in any way?"

"I think it was black," the Earl said vaguely, "with some trimming that might have been red or pink—I really cannot remember. Perhaps your assistant can recall the one I mean."

"That would have been Thalia—I mean Miss Carver," Mrs. Burton said as if to herself. "I will ask her."

49

She crossed the room to speak to Thalia, who disappeared into the back of the shop and returned with the black and red bonnet that the Earl remembered perfectly well. But he had discovered what he wished to know—the little Milliner's name was Thalia Carver!

It was only when she had been promoted to work in the front of the shop that Thalia had been called by her surname prefixed with "Miss."

The work-girls were all addressed by their Christian names, but because she was so popular and so unlike the other assistants, who gave themselves airs when there were no customers present, everyone from Mrs. Burton downwards still called her Thalia.

Lady Adelaide was delighted with the black and red bonnet, and after she had ordered it to be sent to her house and the Earl had told Mrs. Burton to send the bill to him, they left the shop.

He deliberately did not even glance in Thalia's direction, but he was aware that she did not look at him—which for him was an unusual experience.

Now as he drew up his horses outside the shabby door, he thought that she could not help being impressed by his Phaeton if not by him.

As the groom ran to the horses' heads, the Earl climbed down to wait with a feeling that, surprisingly, was nearly one of impatience.

It was a long time, he thought, since he had felt interested in a woman who was not already flirting with him over a supper-table or contriving in the most obvious manner that they should be alone in the Conservatory or the garden of a Mansion in which a Ball was being given.

Last night the two beauties to whom the Princess had introduced him had made it quite clear what they wanted, and he had therefore found himself bored after a very short time in their company.

Some cynical part of his mind told him that the pursuit of the little Milliner would be no different.

At the same time, he could not help remembering that when she had flounced away from him in Genevieve's bedroom she had certainly not shown any eagerness to speak to him again, let alone to meet him.

"I shall undoubtedly find that I have been over-optimistic in expecting her to be any different," he told himself, "although her hair is certainly an unexpected colour for someone of her class."

The shop-door opened and the Earl waited expectantly, but it was not Thalia who came out but a number of other women.

Most of them were middle-aged or elderly, with the exception of two very young girls who, the Earl suspected, were what was known as "matchers" and occupied the lowest and least-paid positions in Mrs. Burton's shop.

Because he always made it his business to know all the details about anything and anyone in whom he was interested, this afternoon when he had left White's he had gone to a book-shop to find out if there were any publications about shops and their assistants.

He had accounts with several book-shops, but the nearest to White's was John Hatchard's at 190 Piccadilly.

He was the bookseller to Queen Charlotte, while Nicoll in Pall Mall was patronised by the King.

As the Earl expected, the shop was filled with a number of men and women from the Social World and a number who were not, most of them talking amongst themselves while they imbibed cups of coffee.

The Earl was immediately recognised by John Hatchard, who hurried to bow his pleasure respectfully at receiving His Lordship in person.

Although he regularly bought a number of books, they were usually ordered by his secretary and delivered to Hellington House.

51

The Earl told John Hatchard what he required.

"That is not a difficult request, My Lord," Mr. Hatchard replied. "I have here William Abbott's *Reminiscences of an Old Draper,* and there is quite a lot about a shopkeeper who ranges from grocer to cheese-monger to Men's-Milliner in *Cranford* by Mrs. Gaskell."

The Earl glanced at the books and decided they would tell him a little of what he wished to know, and he ignored Mr. Hatchard's expostulations when he said that instead of having them delivered he would take them with him.

He had driven back home to peruse what he had bought, and now, seeing the women staring at him with surprise and curiosity as they left the shop, he thought it was unlikely that they had ever had what the servants called a "follower" waiting for them at the back-door.

They continued to turn their heads even when they had reached the end of the street, but the Earl waited, feeling it was unlikely that Thalia would leave by the front.

In this he was correct, for, ten minutes after Mrs. Burton's other employees had left, she stepped out into the street.

She was wearing the concealing grey bonnet which she had worn in Genevieve's bedroom, and because her head was bent as she closed the door behind her, she did not see who was waiting.

It was the horses which caught her eye first, then as her head went up to stare at them the Earl was in front of her, blocking her view.

"Good-evening, Miss Carver!"

For a moment it seemed as if, because she was so astonished to see him, she could not find the words to reply. Then she announced in the low, musical voice he remembered:

"Good-evening, My Lord."

She made an effort to proceed, but with the Earl blocking her way it was not easy.

"I hope," he said, "you will allow me to drive you home. I have brought my Phaeton, as you see, in order to do so."

"I thank Your Lordship, but I have someone waiting for me."

This was certainly not the answer the Earl had expected.

He glanced round, finding that there was no other vehicle in the street except a passing dray and only a few pedestrians.

"I think you are mistaken," he said, "and I can only repeat my invitation. I am very eager, Miss Carver, to drive you home in style."

"It is not an invitation I can accept, My Lord," Thalia said, and the Earl thought there was a deliberately repressive note in her voice.

She stepped to one side of him, and before he could make any effort to stop her, she was walking quickly down the street. He stared after her, not quite certain what he should do.

Then as he watched he saw the figure of an elderly woman dressed in black moving toward her.

They stopped, spoke for a moment, then hurried round the corner.

The Earl climbed back into his Phaeton. He drove in the direction in which Thalia had gone and was just in time to see her turning another corner into Hay Hill.

Again he followed, but this time he encountered a coach-and-four coming down Dover Street, and by the time he had allowed it to precede him he merely had a glimpse of Thalia's grey gown disappearing into Lansdowne Passage.

This, at any rate, told him in which direction she was going, because Lansdowne Passage was a short-cut to Curzon Street.

By the time the Earl had driven through Berkeley Square, passing Lansdowne House, and into Curzon Street, Thalia and her elderly companion were far ahead.

However skilfully he drove, the Earl was brought to the irritating conclusion that he had been outwitted when he saw Thalia turn under the archway which led into Shepherd's Market.

Here it was impossible for his Phaeton to follow her, but at least, he told himself as he drove on up Curzon Street, he knew whereabouts she lived.

He had almost reached the top of the street before he came to a decision.

"Get down, Henry," he said to his groom. "Go to Shepherd's Market and find out all you can about Miss Carver. The place is so small that I cannot believe there will not be someone to give you her address. Discover if she lives alone or has a family. I want every possible detail, but make your enquiries with discretion. I know I can trust you."

"Oi'll be as quick as Oi can, M'Lord," Henry replied.

It was not the first time he had been sent on a strange mission for his employer, and as he was usually the conveyor of notes, flowers, and presents to the ladies in whom the Earl was interested, he referred to himself jokingly when he was among the other servants as "Eros."

"Get along with ye!" the housemaids would say. "Ye ain't got no wings, 'Enry, an' never likely to 'ave!"

"Ye've got no idea what Oi can do with me bow and arrow," Henry would boast.

They would scream with laughter as he chased them round the passages in the basement of Hellington House, only to be reproved by the Butler or the Housekeeper for making a noise.

Now he jumped down from the Phaeton and made his way back towards Shepherd's Market.

Like all His Lordship's staff, he admired the Earl

wholeheartedly not only for his appearance but also because he was an outstanding sportsman, and it was therefore a very enviable position to be in his employment.

The Earl was not aware that all the servants who had been with him since he returned from the war preferred service with a bachelor.

Most of them had found that in a position where their employer had a wife, life was far more arduous, far more difficult, and there was inevitably much less freedom.

The Earl expected everything to be perfect where he was concerned, but he was never niggardly or petty.

There was no-one amongst his servants who had not tales to tell of how difficult their lives could be when there was a nagging mistress or, worse still, a cheese-paring one, in contrast with the tolerance of a good master.

Of one thing Henry was sure—the Earl would not be looking for a wife in Shepherd's Market; in fact, he assumed that he had altogether another position in mind for the girl in grey.

There had been bets in the stables for some time as to how soon the place left empty by the last "bit o' muslin" would be filled.

"Bet her jumps at the chance," Henry said to himself.

* * *

It was after six o'clock when the Earl, reading the newspapers in the Library at Hellington House, was interrupted by the Butler, who said that Henry wished to speak to him.

"Show him in!" the Earl ordered.

Henry came into the room and there was a smile on his face which told the Earl before he spoke that his mission had been successful.

He was a very small and wiry little man who

looked far younger than he actually was, and he had, as the Earl was well aware, an exceptional way with horses.

He was also completely honest, but he had an adventurous streak which, the Earl thought, complemented his own.

He put down the *Morning Post*.

"Well, Henry?"

"Oi've found out all about 'er, M'Lord. 'Er lives at Number Eighty-two, an' a tidy little 'ouse it be."

"Alone?"

"No, M'Lord. 'Er mother lives with 'er an' they tells me 'er's always ill. A Physician comes regular. An' th' woman 'er were with be a servant, M'Lord, name of Hannah—a regular old battle-axe they tells Oi 'er can be when it comes t'shoppin'. Expects th' best cuts for as little as 'er can get 'em."

The Earl smiled.

He was aware that Henry would have made enquiries at the butchers of which there were traditionally a number in Shepherd's Market.

"Anything more, Henry?" he enquired.

"Everyone speaks well o' the young lidy, M'Lord. Said as 'er were 'avin' a 'ard time 'til 'er got a job in Bond Street, but since then 'as paid on th' nail an' never asks for favours like some they could mention!"

The Earl had learnt what he wished to know.

"Thank you, Henry."

"Pleasure, M'Lord!" Henry said cheekily.

With a grin that was an impertinence in itself, he went from the room.

The Earl, who would have permitted no familiarity from any other member of his household, was particularly lenient where Henry was concerned.

He supposed it was because Henry was such a little man. At the same time, he was not only useful but trustworthy and that was something the Earl had found in the war was more important than spit and polish and an unbending conventionality.

Without hurrying himself, the Earl rose to his feet, walked into the Hall, and took his hat and cane from the footman on duty.

"Do you require a carriage, M'Lord?" one of the lackeys enquired.

"No, I am walking," the Earl replied.

He left the house. The south end of Berkeley Square was only a short distance from Shepherd's Market and the Earl knew he would have to proceed on foot in the Market itself.

Although it was late in the afternoon, the small shops were still open as the majority of them catered to those who worked, and they were so individualistic that they had no wish to copy the more important shops which had certain closing hours.

It was obvious that those who shopped in the Market were friendly and in most cases as familiar with one another as if it were really the small country village it had been throughout the centuries.

It was not difficult for the Earl to find Number 82 amongst the modest little dwellings which he suspected were occupied mostly by craftsmen.

As he approached it, he liked what he saw of the curtains that hung at the windows, the cleanliness of the windows themselves, and the way the ancient knocker on the door had been polished until it reflected its surroundings like a mirror.

The Earl raised the knocker with his hand and waited.

There was a pause before he heard footsteps coming down an uncarpeted passage and a moment later the door opened.

The elderly woman who was dressed like a respectable servant, and who he knew had accompanied Thalia home, was looking at him in what was quite obviously a hostile manner.

"I wish to see Miss Carver," the Earl said in a commanding manner which intimidated most people.

"Miss Carver is not at home, M'Lord."

The Earl noted immediately the way he was addressed, and he knew that Thalia must have told the servant who he was when she had seen him speaking to her in the street.

"I think that is not true."

"Miss Carver is not receiving, M'Lord."

There was no doubt now of the aggresesive note in the woman's voice and she was making it clear, in case the Earl was very obtuse, what "not at home" meant.

"I think she will see me," the Earl said firmly.

He stepped forward as he spoke, and because he was so large there was nothing Hannah could do but move backwards.

For a moment she was discomfited. Then, perhaps afraid of being rude to so distinguished a visitor, she opened a door on the left-hand side of the passage and said:

"If Your Lordship will wait in here."

The Earl moved into a small Sitting-Room. It was, he saw, decorated in good taste although there was nothing of any value in the room. But he noted immediately the desk piled with papers, and he wondered if Thalia drew designs before she trimmed her bonnets so skilfully.

He stood waiting, with his back to the fireplace, wondering with a faint smile on his lips what consternation his arrival was causing upstairs.

Then the door opened and Thalia came in.

She had changed her gown, he noticed, for a simple muslin which became her and seemed to accentuate the lights in her hair and the clearness of her skin.

There was no doubt, the Earl thought as he looked at her, that she was lovely, lovelier than anyone he had seen for a long time, and he knew with a sensation almost of triumph that his persistence in finding her had been well worth while.

He was not prepared, however, for the way that

she shut the door behind her and came quite near to him before she spoke. Then she said in a low voice that was barely above a whisper:

"You must not come here! Please leave at once!"

"Leave?" the Earl enquired. "But why?"

"Because my mother must not know that you have called."

The Earl raised his eye-brows.

"Does your mother's disapproval apply only to me?" he enquired. "Or are your other male acquaintances equally unwelcome?"

"I have no male acquaintances," Thalia said. "But Mama would be horrified if she knew you were here."

"Why?" the Earl asked again.

"Because . . ." Thalia began, then stopped. "There is no need for me to make explanations, My Lord. As Hannah told you, I am not at home, and I must ask you to leave."

"I have no wish to do so," the Earl said. "I want to talk to you, Miss Carver."

"We have nothing to say to each other."

"That is for me to decide, and quite frankly I have a great deal to say."

Thalia looked up to the ceiling as if she was afraid his voice would be overheard. Then again she was pleading with him:

"Please go! It will upset Mama and she is not well. She has so many troubles already, and if she knew . . . you were . . . here, it would perturb her . . . greatly."

"Then of course I must leave," the Earl said, "but as you will understand, as we cannot talk here we must meet somewhere."

"That is impossible!" Thalia said quickly.

"Then I must insist upon staying."

She made what was a stifled cry of annoyance.

"You cannot be so . . . unfeeling when I have told you that my mother is . . . ill."

"Then where can we talk?" the Earl persisted.

There was a sound upstairs and again Thalia looked up at the ceiling before she said frantically:

"Anywhere ... anywhere but ... here!"

"Very well," the Earl said, "I will collect you at half-after-eight o'clock, and we will dine somewhere quiet and discreet where we can talk without being overheard."

Thalia opened her eyes in sheer surprise until they seemed so large they almost filled her face.

"D-dine with you ... alone?"

"I was not thinking of inviting anybody else."

"But of course I ... cannot do such a thing. It would be ... wrong."

"Then let us talk here," the Earl said genially. "You are well chaperoned, even though your mother is on another floor."

"You are blackmailing me," Thalia said after a moment.

"Yes, I am!" the Earl replied. "And let me tell you, I always get what I want, so it would be easier to give in at the beginning and allow me to have my way."

"What can you ... possibly have to ... say to me?"

"That will take time," the Earl said, "but as I have told you, I am ready to say what must be said now, if you will permit me to do so."

He knew that she was agitated, apprehensive, and a little afraid not of him but of the effect his presence would have on her mother.

He knew she was considering, thinking, trying to find a way out of the position in which she found herself.

Then once again a slight noise overheard seemed to make up her mind for her.

"Very well," she said at length, "you have forced my hand and I hate you for doing so. Because I cannot have Mama upset at this ... moment, I will dine with you. But not until after nine o'clock, when she goes to sleep."

"I will call at fifteen minutes past nine," the Earl replied.

"Do not knock on the door," Thalia instructed him. "Just wait outside until I can join you."

He smiled in acknowledgement of her instructions. Then as if she was extremely anxious to get rid of him, she moved to the door and stepped into the small passage outside, to open the front-door.

"Nine-fifteen," the Earl said. "I am prepared to wait quite patiently, Miss Carver, if you are unexpectedly delayed."

Thalia did not answer but merely shut the door, and the Earl had the feeling that if she had been able to act naturally she would have slammed it.

He was smiling as he walked away.

He thought that he had won what had been quite a skirmish—not a battle, that would come later—but definitely a trial of strength in which, as was to be expected, he was the conqueror.

*   *   *

When the Earl had gone, Thalia had stood for a moment in the passage composing herself before she went upstairs.

She was so incensed with the Earl that she felt her mother might easily be aware of the vibrations of anger which she was sure she was sending out almost like sparks of fire.

How dare he follow her here! How dare a man she had seen only once—twice, if one counted his coming to the shop to buy a bonnet for some woman he fancied—force himself upon her in such an ungentlemanly manner?

And to blackmail her into dining with him when she knew it was something she should not do, and which would doubtless give her mother a heart-attack if she ever learnt of it!

Barbara Cartland

"What can I do?" Thalia asked herself.

She had an uncomfortable feeling that if she refused to join him when he came to fetch her, he might easily knock on the door until either she or Hannah opened it, and make a scene if she refused to join him.

"It is impossible! He is behaving in a most un-gentlemanly manner!" she stormed.

Then she realised that it was because he was not treating her as a lady.

She supposed that this was the type of difficulty shop-assistants often encountered, and perhaps for the first time she understood a little of her mother's apprehension that she should pretend to belong to a class inferior to her own.

She took several deep breaths as if to calm herself, then walked slowly up the stairs.

Lady Caversham watched her enter the room.

"Who was it, dearest?" she asked. "Hannah said there was somebody at the door who wished to see you."

There was a note in her mother's voice which told Thalia that she was already worried and a little apprehensive.

Just for a moment she thought of telling her the truth and asking her advice, but she saw how frail her mother looked and knew that any more anxiety, any more worry, might prove disastrous.

It was enough for her to lie awake night after night crying helplessly for her husband, without adding yet another problem to the ones with which they were already beset.

Any further aggravation might be enough to prove fatal.

Thalia made up her mind.

"Actually, Mama, I have had a secret for a long time," she said, "but now I am going to tell you what I have been keeping from you."

"Keeping from me?" Lady Caversham repeated.

"I hope it will make you feel proud of me," Thalia said. "I have written a book!"

"Written a book!" Lady Caversham replied in sheer astonishment.

"Only a very small one," Thalia said. "I was going to wait until your birthday on Friday and give it to you as a present, but as I cannot bottle it up any longer, you must have it now! Wait, Mama, while I fetch it."

As she spoke, Thalia rose to cross the passage from her mother's room to her own.

The author's copies of her book, which she had collected yesterday from Hatchard's after she had been with *Mademoiselle* Genevieve, were in a little pile on her dressing-table.

One had already been wrapped in tissue paper and tied with a bow of pink ribbon.

She had intended to give it, with a number of other small presents, to her mother on her birthday, but she knew now that she must at all costs divert her attention from the Earl's intrusion, and she could think of no better way to do so.

She carried the wrapped book back to the bedroom and put it into her mother's hands.

"There you are, Mama," she said, "your daughter's debut into the Literary World, and I am praying, as you must, that it will be a success and make us a lot of money."

"I cannot believe it!" Lady Caversham exclaimed.

She undid the ribbon with fingers that trembled and pulled the book out of its wrapping.

" *'Gentlemen, by a Person of Quality,'* " she read aloud. "Thalia, what have you written?"

"It was a book I saw in the Library at home that made me think of it," Thalia replied. "It was in French and it was called simply *Les Femmes*. It was a book of sayings which a Frenchman had collected about women all through the ages."

"I think I remember it," Lady Caversham said.

"I showed it to Papa. He laughed and said he could add a great deal to it if he chose and perhaps one day he would write a book about all the women he had known, none of whom were as beautiful as you, Mama."

"Darling Denzil, did he really say that?" Lady Caversham asked.

"He was always saying it," Thalia said. "When I was wondering how I could possibly make money, I remembered *Les Femmes* and thought I would do the same about gentlemen."

"You have written this all yourself?"

"It is not very long," Thalia said modestly.

"How did you get it published?"

"I went to see Mr. John Hatchard at his shop in Piccadilly. I knew he published George Crabbe, and although my work is very different, I asked him if he would read my manuscript. He said he would, and he was so kind to me, Mama. But do you know what he told me about himself?"

"What did he say?" Lady Caversham asked.

"He said that when he opened his book-shop he wrote in his diary: '*This day, by the grace of God, the goodwill of my friends, and five pounds in my pocket, I have opened my book-shop in Piccadilly.*' Just think of it, Mama. He took such a gamble on his shop being a success."

"It was certainly a brave action," Lady Caversham agreed.

"When I told him how very important it was for me to make some money," Thalia went on, "I think he thought of his own struggles and wanted to help me."

"It was very kind of him to publish it when you are unknown," Lady Caversham said. "But this book does not really seem like you, dearest, and I should have thought you might have written a novel."

"I am no Jane Austen," Thalia laughed, "and Mr. Hatchard said he was sure this book would amuse the *Beau Monde*. I am keeping my fingers crossed, Mama, hoping that it makes a lot of money and I become a success overnight like Lord Byron."

Lady Caversham was staring at the book she held in her hand.

"I can hardly believe it," she said. "It seems only the other day that I was teaching you the alphabet and you were trying to read the words of two syllables. Now you have written a book, but I wish you could have put your name on it."

"I would have liked that too," Thalia said, "but Mr. Hatchard said he thought a lot of people would think it impertinent for a woman to criticise gentlemen, and he also thought it would sell better if it had an air of mystery about it."

"I shall read every word," Lady Caversham promised, "and as I do so I shall think what a clever daughter I have."

She looked down at the book again, then asked:

"How could you know so much about men?"

"I suppose the answer is that I know very little, but I remember the things Papa used to say and the witty sayings in many books I have read. Then the idea came to me when I was listening to what the customers said about their husbands and their young men."

"You mean they actually discuss such things in front of you?" Lady Caversham said in a shocked voice.

"Of course, Mama," Thalia answered. "You know people always behave as if servants are deaf. Well, in the eyes of those who buy bonnets, I am only a servant."

She was not listening as her mother started once again to say how much she disliked her being in such an inferior position and working for a living.

Instead, she was wondering what the Earl thought of her and why he was so insistent that he must see her.

When he had come into *Mademoiselle* Genevieve's bedroom looking so tall and elegant she had thought that it was quite obvious why he was there, and from what Genevieve had said before he arrived, Thalia had known that she was expecting an important gentleman to call on her.

Then, surprisingly, this afternoon the Earl had come into the shop with Lady Adelaide, who, according to Mrs. Burton, was one of the beauties of Society and whatever she wore set a fashion amongst the other ladies who all envied her.

When he could have such gorgeous creatures to engage his attention, why on earth should the Earl want to talk to her?

Thalia suddenly had a terrifying idea that he might have discovered who she was, then she told herself that that was absurd.

Why should anyone ever connect Thalia Carver, a Milliner in Bond Street, with Sir Denzil Caversham?

No, that was not the explanation, but she supposed she would learn what it was when she dined with him.

Although she told herself that the Earl was utterly despicable for forcing her to do something which she knew would shock and horrify her mother, she could not help but feel slightly excited at going out to dinner.

Ever since they had come to London, Thalia had become so used to playing the part she had set herself that she was not expecting to have any social life.

She knew her mother was right in saying that they must avoid all the friends they had ever known, not only because it was impossible to give an explanation as to why Sir Denzil had disappeared but also because they had no wish for sympathy or pity.

"When your Papa returns," Lady Caversham had said often enough, "we will first go to the country and live quietly until all the gossip has died down, then we will take up our lives where they left off."

"How will we pay for it, Mama?" Thalia asked.

"Perhaps your father will have some money when he comes home," Lady Caversham replied weakly.

Thalia had thought it very unlikely, knowing that her father had a genius for spending money but none for acquiring it.

She did not, however, wish to make her mother more depressed than she was already, so she merely said:

"I am sure Papa is clever enough to put everything to . . . rights, even our finances."

Lady Caversham ate her supper, brought up to her on a tray, and because she was so interested in Thalia's book she managed to eat more than usual.

"You have been very good this evening, Mama," Thalia said with satisfaction, "and you must not forget to tell Hannah how much you enjoyed the new way she cooked the chicken."

"Was it chicken?" Lady Caversham asked vaguely, then said quickly: "Of course I will. Dear Hannah tries so hard to tempt my appetite. I feel so ashamed because I am never hungry."

"Perhaps the book will bring in lots of money," Thalia said, "then we can tempt you with all sorts of exquisite delicacies. You might even, like the Romans, fancy peacock-tongues."

Lady Caversham gave a little cry of horror.

"How could they be so cruel?"

"I was only teasing, Mama," Thalia said quickly. "You are feeling much better this evening, but I want you to try to go to sleep and not read my book as I know you are longing to do."

"I would be much happier for us to read it together."

"We will do that tomorrow," Thaila murmured, "but now I am going to help you into bed. Then I will just read you a few extracts to make you laugh."

By the time Lady Caversham was in bed, having laughed over some of the things Thalia had written, it was past nine o'clock.

After kissing her mother good-night, Thalia went to her own bedroom. She told herself that if His Lordship was expecting her to be wearing evening-dress, he was going to be disappointed.

She did not possess one.

She had been fifteen when her father had left England and since then the only new gown she had had was one which she and Hannah had made together.

Recently they had found some cheap but attractive muslin in the market and there were ribbons too, not the expensive satin ones which during the war were smuggled in from France, but in pretty colours, although they creased easily.

Thalia washed and changed into her latest gown simply because the rest were almost in rags.

It was a sprigged muslin with two frills on the bottom of the skirt and a frill round the neck which made her look very young.

"If he expects someone sophisticated," Thalia told her reflection in the mirror, "he should take out Lady Adelaide!"

Then she told herself that she was presuming very much on the idea that the Earl was asking her to dine because he thought of her as a woman.

She could not help feeling that he had a very different reason, and again Thalia asked herself a little apprehensively what it could be.

As she arranged her hair, she realised that it was

already twenty-minutes past nine and doubtless the Earl was waiting.

"Let him wait!" she told herself savagely, then was afraid he might put his threat into operation and knock loudly on the door, disturbing her mother.

Like many people who are ill, Lady Caversham had a habit of dropping off almost immediately when she went to bed, only to awaken two or three hours later and find it impossible to sleep again.

To be disturbed early in the evening was disastrous, for that meant she would have what was described as a "white night" and in the morning would seem so frail that Thalia would be afraid.

'I must go down to him,' she thought.

She took from the wardrobe a long cloak which her mother had worn in the days when they were more affluent.

It was of velvet in a deep madonna blue and had once been trimmed with sable before Thalia had sold the fur to provide themselves with something to eat.

It was simple and hung over her shoulders, making her, with the strange colour of her hair, appear as if she had stepped out of a stained-glass window.

To herself she merely looked somewhat underdressed, but she thought that if the Earl was ashamed of her, there was nothing she could do about it.

She tip-toed quietly down the stairs and went into the kitchen.

Hannah looked at her and her face darkened.

"What's the world coming to, that's what I'd like to know!" she said. "He's no right to ask you out alone. You know that!"

"I do know it, Hannah," Thalia answered, "but what else could I do? I could not have him upset Mama."

"I suppose you could have insisted I come with you," Hannah said grudgingly.

Just for a moment Thalia thought it would be amusing to see the Earl's reaction to this request. Then she said aloud:

"That is what I would like to do, but supposing Mama should wake and find nobody in the house?"

"I only hopes as you can manage a man like His Lordship," Hannah said grimly, "but I doubts it."

Thalia rather doubted it too, but she asked herself what was the alternative.

Hannah gave a sudden cry.

"What is it?" Thalia asked.

"I've an idea! I've an idea, Miss Thalia! Just you wait here."

As she spoke she went from the kitchen down the stairs which led to the cellar.

Thalia looked after her in perplexity.

She knew there was nothing in the cellar except for the trunks they had brought with them from the country, a number of which belonged to her father and contained his clothes.

When they had unpacked, there had been nowhere to put his things in so small a house and Hannah had therefore put them in the cellar to unpack them from time to time to make certain they were not being spoilt by dampness or moths.

Thalia waited, aware that the Earl was waiting too and doubtless growing more and more impatient.

Then Hannah came heavily up the narrow staircase from the cellar.

"Here's what I was looking for," she said. "You take it with you, Miss Thalia. You might find it useful."

She held out her hand as she spoke, and when Thalia saw what was in it she gave a little gasp.

"A pistol, Hannah!"

"It's your Papa's, and it's loaded. I could only find one bullet, so if you have to use it, you have only one chance."

70

"I cannot! I cannot take it!" Thalia said. "It was because Papa shot a man that we are in this situation now."

"I know that," Hannah said stolidly, "but there's worse things to be afraid of than fire-arms. You take this pistol with you, Miss Thalia, in case you need it."

Thalia knew she was talking sense.

She also realised that the pistol was a very small one, which she now remembered her father had carried in the evening when he drove some distance to a party.

There were always Highwaymen and footpads to be wary of in every part of the country.

Although Thalia did not remember their ever being held up or robbed, there were always stories of other people who had had unpleasant experiences when, with nothing with which to defend themselves, they had been obliged meekly to hand over their valuables.

It struck her that she might be in the same position—obliged to do anything the Earl demanded of her because she would be quite unable to fight him . . . if that was how their evening ended.

"Perhaps you are right, Hannah," she said. "It is always wise to be prepared."

She took the pistol from the maid and put it in the satin bag she carried, which was attached to her arm by ribbons.

It was heavy, but at least she thought it unlikely that the Earl would be aware of it, and she thought that if she opened the bag to obtain her handkerchief, she must be careful that he did not see what was inside.

"Now I must go," she said.

Hannah did not reply. She merely walked stolidly and slowly ahead of her as if, Thalia thought with a hint of amusement, she were taking her to her execution instead of to the front-door.

It was just beginning to grow dark but it was quite easy to see the Earl standing a little way up the road.

As Thalia walked towards him she was aware that he was looking particularly resplendent in an evening-cloak thrown back over one shoulder.

Beneath it he was wearing full evening-dress with the exception that instead of knee-breeches, he had on the long "drain-pipe" trousers which had just been introduced as a new fashion.

As Thalia reached him, she was aware how insignificant and nondescript she must appear in contrast.

"You are late!" the Earl said without any formal acknowledgement of her presence. "I was just beginning to wonder if I should have to remind you I was outside by knocking on the door."

"I was afraid you might do that. That is why I am here."

"Your mother is not aware that you have left the house?"

"No."

He stood looking at her, and Thalia said suddenly:

"You have won your bet, My Lord, or perhaps it was just a challenge you set yourself. Now may I go back? There is no point in your giving me dinner, for, as you can well see, I am unable even to dress the part."

"You look charming!" the Earl said in a voice that was impersonal. "But if you are afraid of who might see you, we are going somewhere very quiet, where I can talk to you as I wish to do."

Thalia did not reply and he said:

"My carriage is waiting in Curzon Street. I think this is the quickest way to join it."

As he spoke, he put his hand under her elbow and started to move in the direction he wished to go, and Thalia, feeling that there was no point in arguing any further, went with him.

Many of the shops in Shepherd's Market were still open and there were a few customers, mostly chatting with the shop-keepers rather than buying.

But otherwise the place seemed almost deserted and Thalia had the feeling that she was walking in a dream as they came from the shadows of the archway into the bright gas-lights of Curzon Street.

There was a closed carriage waiting, embellished with the Earl's crest and drawn by two horses with a coachman and a footman in attendance.

She stepped inside, and as the Earl joined her she thought for a moment that she had moved back into the past.

It was her father's carriage in which she was riding, and there was no tragedy, no years of worry and privation, no heart-searching as to where the next meal would come from.

She was for the moment so deep in thought that she did not realise that the Earl, leaning back comfortably in the corner of the carriage, was watching her with a look of amusement, until he asked:

"What are you thinking about so seriously?"

"Myself," Thalia answered. "Forgive me for being inattentive, but for the moment I find it an absorbing subject."

It struck the Earl that any other woman would have told him that she had been thinking of him.

"At least you are honest, Miss Carver," he said. "Most people think incessantly about themselves but are not frank enough to say so."

"I always tell the truth if it is possible," Thalia replied. "It is so much less of a struggle. I am ashamed tonight that I am deceiving my mother, whom I love very deeply, by being here with you."

"As she will not know you are deceiving her," the Earl said, "I cannot feel that there is any very great damage; and if we are going to have a pleasant evening, Miss Carver, I suggest we omit any recriminations, which invariably bore me."

"I was not aware that my duty this evening is to prevent you from being bored or to keep you entertained, My Lord."

"You are doing that already," the Earl said, "by not telling me, as effusively as I expect, how much you are looking forward to being in my company."

"As I have already said, I try always to tell the truth," Thalia replied, "and you know without my saying so that I have no wish for your company but would much rather be at home in bed with a good book."

"Is that what you do every night?"

"Yes."

"That is certainly extremely wasteful of your youth and of course your looks."

"But not my brain?"

"You consider that of more importance than your more obvious assets?"

"Naturally, and more lasting."

The Earl laughed.

"You are certainly original in that contention, if it is indeed the truth, but perhaps spending your time with women who think only of their outward appearance has caused you personally to concentrate on something different.

"I feel sorry for a lot of them."

"Why?" the Earl enquired.

"Because they have been brought up to believe that the only thing that matters is to attract men. That is why they buy bonnets, why they spend hours choosing materials, ribbons, face-creams, shoes, stockings, sun-shades. There is no end to what they believe will be the bait to catch a fish."

"Like myself?" the Earl asked.

"But of course!" Thalia agreed. "The Earl of Hellington would be a very large catch if they could land him!"

"I assure you, I fight ferociously never to be netted."

"That I can well believe," Thalia said, "but shall I be prophetic and tell Your Lordship you will be caught in the end and once you are in the net there will be no escape?"

"That is exactly what I am afraid of," the Earl said. "At the same time, perhaps you are right. It is nature's way that a man should be caught and captured and made a fool of by some determined woman. Think how Adam suffered through Eve!"

"And from all I have heard, he has never stopped whining about it ever since!" Thalia added.

She spoke with a stringent little note in her voice which made the Earl laugh.

"When you take off your grey disguise, Miss Carver, I see you are very different from the demure creature who spoke softly and almost ingratiatingly to her client."

"Do I sound like that?" Thalia asked. "That is interesting."

"Why?"

"Because the Egyptians believed in the power of the voice, and I have often wondered how much a voice counts in the modern world."

She thought for a moment, then she said:

"In the Army it obviously galvanises a soldier into action because he has been trained to obey, but perhaps if used more hypnotically it can control ordinary people who are not trained to listen."

"It is certainly an interesting contention," the Earl said, "and one we must certainly pursue further. But as you see, we have now arrived at our destination."

Thalia looked out the window to see that the horses had drawn up outside a large building lit by gas-lamps which gave it a garish appearance.

At first she could only stare, then she said in a small, rather frightened voice:

"No-no . . . I cannot go . . . there!"

"It is all right," the Earl said soothingly, "you will not be seen. We are dining in a private room."

It struck Thalia that that was certainly not the sort of place she should go alone with a man.

She had read of private rooms. Casanova, the Marquise de Sade, and all sorts of other rapacious creatures in history had taken the women they wished to seduce to private rooms in different parts of Europe, but she did not know they existed in London.

But if it was not a private room here, it was, she told herself practically, sure to be a private room somewhere else, and she was no more likely to be safe in the Earl's house, in which she had somehow expected they might dine, than she would be anywhere else.

The footman opened the door and the Earl stepped out to help her alight.

Just for a moment she hesitated, then as she moved her arm she felt the heaviness of her bag and found it extremely reassuring.

Chapter Four

As the waiters withdrew, the Earl sat back in his chair with a glass of brandy in his hand.

He thought as he looked at Thalia sitting opposite him that the dinner had been unexpectedly stimulating and interesting. In fact he could not remember when he had last had such an intelligent conversation with a man, and he knew he had never had one with a woman.

Their conversation had ranged over a great number of subjects and he had become aware that Thalia was exceedingly well read and also had an original turn of mind.

She looked very young, but he thought he might in fact have been talking to Lady Melbourne or Lady Holland, very much older women who were noted in the *Beau Monde* for their intelligence.

For Thalia it had been a fascinating experience to talk with a man who, she realised, was very unlike the empty-headed *Beaux* who came into Mrs. Burton's shop and chattered inanely while their ladies fitted on bonnets.

She had often wondered what it would be like to dine with a man alone and to find herself free to express the opinions which she had kept very much to herself these last three years.

Many of the Tutors under whom she had studied

in London, and there had been several, had told her almost reproachfully that she had a man's brain and it was not what they expected to find in a woman.

With her father she had been able to talk about a great number of things but was subject to the handicap that Sir Denzil was not a good listener and preferred his own opinions to other people's.

Her mother, on the other hand, was an excellent listener, but although Thalia adored her, she had to be honest and admit that her mother was not interested in anything that did not particularly touch her personal life.

Perhaps one of the reasons why she and her husband had been so happy together was the fact that while he talked, she was completely content to listen and she thought that everything he said was wonderful.

But the Earl was undoubtedly a much cleverer man, though Thalia thought he was somewhat dogmatic in what he asserted, and he was obviously surprised if ever she disagreed with him.

They had several spirited arguments, but it was only now, when there were no longer any servants in the room, that she looked round her and was conscious of her surroundings.

She had in fact, when she had first entered the place where the Earl was giving her dinner, been apprehensive.

There were the sounds of music and voices and there were a number of servants standing about in crimson uniforms heavily over-trimmed with gold braid.

Then to her relief they were escorted up a staircase which led to the first floor and shown into a room where there was a table laid only for two.

'If this is a private room,' Thalia thought, 'then it is not what I expected.'

She had always had a picture in her mind of something gaudy and rather vulgar, but this room was decorated in the French fashion in discreet good taste.

There were a number of French prints on the walls, a sofa and several chairs covered in brocade, and at one end of the room where Thalia thought there must be windows, there were curtains of a very attractive turquoise blue.

She thought to herself that it was the blue that François Boucher had used in his pictures, and somehow, because it was so different from what she had anticipated, it was reassuring.

The Earl took her cloak from her shoulders and she was tense because he was touching her. Then because he did it in a manner which had nothing but politeness about it, she felt at ease as she sat down on the sofa.

"A glass of champagne, or would you prefer Madeira?" the Earl enquired.

Thalia hesitated.

"It is a very long time since I tasted either."

"Then I think it should be champagne," the Earl suggested.

The waiter handed Thalia a glass, from which she took only a tiny sip, knowing that it would be a very great mistake if she became muddle-minded from alcohol and remembering that it was hours since she had eaten anything.

Hannah always packed her a light luncheon to take with her to eat in the work-room at Mrs. Burton's shop.

Some of the women would go out for a little while at midday to buy themselves food from the stalls that were always to be found in side-streets or just to stretch their legs.

But Thalia had promised her mother that she would go nowhere alone, and in fact she had no wish to do so. Besides which, there was always far too much to do in the work-room.

She was well aware that because she was so skilful at trimming the bonnets, Mrs. Burton made her do the work of two people, and she not only trimmed the fashionable creations she made so skilfully but also sold them.

The dinner she had eaten with the Earl had been rich and delicious, and Thalia was now wondering how she could explain to Hannah what had been on the menu so that she could copy for her mother some of the things she had enjoyed.

"Is there anything else you would like?" the Earl asked.

"It would be impossible to eat any more!" Thalia replied. "I only wish I were a camel, then I would not have to eat for at least a week after such a delicious dinner."

"You are too thin," the Earl said. "Is that because you wish to be fashionable or because you usually do not have enough to eat?"

"I have enough now that I am fortunate in being able to earn the money with which to buy the food."

"I cannot believe that Mrs. Burton is over-generous."

Thalia smiled.

"I am told she is typical of all the Bond Street shop-keepers who extract astronomical sums from their clients but pay their work-people as little as possible."

"That is what I thought," the Earl said, "and I have another proposition to put to you."

"Proposition?" Thalia asked.

He looked at her for a long moment before he said:

"You must be aware that a Milliner's is not the right background for anyone as lovely as yourself."

He saw Thalia's eyes widen in surprise and he went on:

"Are you going to be so mock-modest as to tell me you are not aware of your beauty?"

"Of course I should like to think I am beautiful," Thalia answered, "but when I compare myself with the acknowledged beauties who come to the shop, like the one you were with today, or indeed with *Mademoiselle* Genevieve, I am well aware of my deficiencies."

"If you have any, I cannot see them."

Because the Earl spoke with that cynical note in his voice that was characteristic of him, it was difficult to take what he was saying as a compliment.

Thalia gave a little laugh as she said:

"Anyway, I have learnt it is a handicap to be thought too attractive when one is only a shop-assistant. As Your Lordship might have been aware, I am allowed to wait only on the old and the plain, not on the Ladies of Quality who bring their admirers with them."

"And yet you were permitted to visit a ballet-dancer."

"That was different," Thalia replied. "A person like *Mademoiselle* Genevieve is not likely to notice somebody as insignificant as myself. But actually it was the first time I was sent on such an errand, and I hope it will be the last."

She spoke so positively that the Earl questioned in surprise:

"Why do you say that?"

"Because although a ballet-dancer may not notice me, the gentlemen who frequent her dressing-room undoubtedly do so, like yourself, My Lord," Thalia answered. "If I had not gone to Fletcher's Hotel, I would not be here at this moment."

"Then I am glad you did so," the Earl said.

There was a little pause which, for some reason she did not understand, made Thalia feel embarrassed.

It might have been because of the way the Earl

81

was looking at her, scrutinising her, she thought, as a man might scrutinise a picture or a horse, almost as if he were appraising and evaluating her points.

"I think, My Lord," she said, "while I must thank you for that delicious dinner, it is now time for me to go home."

"Not yet," the Earl said sharply. "I have not yet told you of my proposition."

"I will of course listen to what you have to say, but I would remind you that it is getting late."

"Not as far as I am concerned."

"But you do not have to get up as early as I do," Thalia remarked.

"Very well then, you have made your point," the Earl said. "Listen carefully . . ."

Thalia bent forward, put her arms on the table, and rested her chin in her hands.

Her bag was in her lap and she thought she must remember not to rise quickly, otherwise it would fall to the floor with a clatter.

"I think we agree," the Earl said, "that you are in the wrong environment. What I am going to suggest is that you move to a larger house in a quieter locality and that you allow me to make you very much more comfortable than you are at the moment.

"You will not have to make the bonnets you wear, you can have your own carriage and two horses to drive you, and you will certainly need one if not two servants to wait on you."

He spoke in the same voice that he had used all evening, quiet and clear, with just a faint note of cynicism which made everything he said seem somehow impersonal.

He stopped speaking and realised that Thalia was looking at him incredulously, then she said:

"Is that . . . all?"

"All?" the Earl questioned. "What else would you like me to add? Jewels? A box at Covent Garden?"

"I did not mean it like that," Thalia said. "It is

just impossible to believe that what Your Lordship is saying is not some strange jest."

The Earl frowned.

"Jest! Why should you think that?"

Thalia linked her fingers together and, sitting up very straight, looked at him.

"Unless I am mistaken, My Lord . . . and perhaps I am . . . I think, although it seems highly . . . improbable, that you are inviting me to become your . . . mistress."

"That was my intention," the Earl said.

"Do gentlemen really make such suggestions in the same business-like way that you have approached me?"

"Did you expect something different?"

"But of course!" Thalia answered. "I imagined that a man would burn with a fiery passion and address the object of his fancy with heart-rending eloquence."

She paused before adding:

"Alternatively, he could threaten her with a closure of the mortgage or whatever else is traditionally held over women on such occasions."

Looking at Thalia, the Earl saw the two dimples he had noticed before at the corners of her mouth and was aware that she was laughing at him.

"I have a feeling," he said, "that you are not taking me seriously."

"How could I?" she asked. "I have never heard such a ridiculous proposition in my life! If that is the reason why you brought me out to dinner, My Lord, all I can say is that Hannah need not have been afraid of what might happen to me."

"I thought, perhaps wrongly," the Earl said, "that before we entered into an agreement together you would wish to know what to expect."

"I have told you what I expect."

"A fiery passion?" the Earl questioned. "That, of course, comes later."

"I am glad you have warned me," Thalia replied, "but now, My Lord, I really must go home."

"You have not yet given me an answer."

"Do you expect one?"

"But of course. I am not in the habit of asking questions and receiving no answers."

"Then let me make it plain, My Lord, so that it is impossible for you to misunderstand me—the answer is an unqualified 'No!'"

"Can you really be so foolish?" the Earl asked. "Have you thought of the advantages I can offer you?"

"It may come as a surprise to Your Lordship, but nothing you have said so far seems to offer me any advantage over what I have already."

"And what is that?" the Earl asked.

"My self-respect," Thalia replied, "and that, My Lord, is something it is not in your power to give."

The Earl put down his glass.

"Shall I approach you in another way?" he said after a moment. "Shall I tell you how very desirable I find you and how much I would like to look after you and do everything within my power to make you happy?"

"That you can do now."

"How?"

He had the feeling, as he spoke, that her reply would not be what he wished to hear.

"By leaving me alone," Thalia said. "You are well aware that you have blackmailed me into coming here tonight, simply because I could not upset my mother. That is something which must not happen again."

She saw an expression that she thought was one of annoyance on the Earl's face and could not resist adding:

"As for your house, your carriage, your horses, and your jewels, I am certain *Mademoiselle* Genevieve will accept all those and a great deal more with pleasure!"

"I am not interested in Genevieve but in you!"

"For which you obviously think I should be flattered and grateful. I am neither! When I think it over I shall find your proposition, My Lord . . . insulting!"

"It was not meant to be that."

Thalia made a little gesture with her hands.

"How can you expect me to think anything else?"

The Earl did not reply and after a moment she said:

"I know exactly what you are thinking, My Lord. You are wondering how anyone so inferior, so unimportant as an underpaid Milliner can refuse the Earl of Hellington. Well, I am not only refusing you but making it very clear that I consider, despite your intelligence, that you are a very bad judge of character."

If she had tried she could not have said anything to annoy the Earl more.

If there was one thing on which he had always prided himself, it was that he could sum up a man the moment he talked to him.

He did not require references for his servants, and when people came to him with an appeal for help he could tell the moment he met them whether or not they were genuine.

Now, that this chit of a girl, with no background and nothing except her beauty to distinguish her from thousands of women like her, should consider that he had insulted her, and at the same time accuse him of bad judgement in making his offer in the first place, almost took his breath away.

"Now listen to me, Thalia," he began, only to be interrupted as Thalia replied:

"I have listened to you, My Lord, and really there is nothing more to say on the subject. If you want the truth, I find it extremely boring to go on discussing it."

As she spoke, she picked up her bag and rose

to her feet, looking, although she was unaware of it, alluring and at the same time very young and un-touched in the candle-light.

Thalia had been so intent on talking to the Earl that she had not realised that when the waiters left the room they had extinguished all the lights ex-cept for the four candles on the dining-table.

There was, however, another light, and only as Thalia turned from the table did she become aware of it.

She had been sitting with her back to the cur-tains at the end of the room which she supposed con-cealed a window. Now they were slightly drawn back and she saw no window but another room in which was a bed.

There was a small chandelier containing three candles at the side of one of the curtains which draped the bed. There were lace-edged pillows and on the bed was a cover of frilly pink, also a Bouch-er colour, decorated with love-knots and turquoise-blue ribbons.

For a moment Thalia stood as if turned to stone. Then she moved towards her cloak, which was lying on a chair beside the sofa.

Only as she reached it did she realise that while she had left the table the Earl had not moved.

He was watching her from the high-backed chair in which he had sat at dinner and once again he held his glass in his hand.

"I wish to go, My Lord."

"Supposing I do not let you?"

"I think you would find it . . . difficult to . . . prevent me."

"Do you really believe that?"

"Yes. At the same time, I should be very disap-pointed."

"Disappointed?" the Earl questioned.

"When I was talking to you at dinner I thought you were not only intelligent but also a gentleman in the correct sense of the word. I would not wish to be disillusioned."

"That sounds very plausible, Thalia, and what I might have expected from you," the Earl said. "At the same time, since you have made it clear that you have no wish to see me again, what you feel about me after tonight can hardly be of any particular consequence."

As Thalia sought for a reply, she thought that once again they were arguing as they had at dinner, almost as if they fought a duel with clever words.

Because she could find no ready answer, she bent down and picked up her cloak and put it over her shoulders.

"I intend to leave, My Lord," she said. "Are you going to stop me by brute force? That, as you must know, is the last resort of an animal without brains."

"No, I will not make that sort of attempt to stop you," the Earl replied, "but shall I say instead that I will call on you tomorrow, and if you are not back from the shop where you enjoy working, then perhaps I will discuss the alternative situation I have offered you with your mother."

Thalia gave a little gasp, then with her eyes blazing with anger she walked back towards the table.

"That is the most underhanded, dirty, caddish type of blackmail any man could stoop to use!"

She stood at the table almost spitting the words at him and the Earl laughed.

"You look very lovely when you are angry," he said, "and I could not resist seeing your eyes flashing, as I assure you they do, and hearing you denounce me!"

"You were not ... really ... threatening me?"

"No. I would not sink to that level."

"Then why did you frighten me?" Thalia asked. "You know how vulnerable I am where Mama is concerned."

"Just as I am vulnerable where you are concerned."

"You can hardly expect me to believe that after the way you have behaved."

"How have I behaved?" the Earl asked. "Except when just a few minutes ago I obeyed an irresistible impulse to make you angry."

Thalia did not reply and he said:

"I merely offered you something I thought you would find more enjoyable than struggling as you are now to keep yourself, your mother, and doubtless your maid, Hannah, alive. You have refused me! Very well, we must start again. I must find something that you will accept."

He was aware that Thalia was looking at him uncertainly, not understanding his change of mood, and he went on reflectively:

"Perhaps it would be special treatment for your mother and the very best Doctors in London to diagnose her condition."

"That is also unfair . . . and you know it!" Thalia cried.

" 'All is fair in love and war,' " the Earl quoted.

"Love!" Thalia exclaimed derisively. "That is the first time you have mentioned love! But you cannot use that word in connection with your . . . proposition."

"So that is what you want."

"Of course I want love," Thalia retorted, "but that is something you could never give me, My Lord, so there is no point in our talking about it."

"I see I have been, as you so rightly point out, extremely stupid," the Earl said.

There was a twist to his lips as he added:

"How could I have forgotten that a woman always wants to be wooed?"

"That is the last thing I want," Thalia said sharply. "If by wooing you mean an attempt to persuade

me by some...devious method to accept the...
things I have just...refused."

"But if they were yours you would appreciate
them all the same," the Earl said shrewdly.

"I have always heard that one should beware of
Greeks when they come bearing gifts," Thalia said,
"and forewarned is forearmed My Lord. Whatever
you offer me now, I shall be well aware of the
ulterior motive behind it."

"Then I shall have to think out my campaign
from another angle."

Thalia gave a little laugh.

"So that is what I am—a campaign! The battle
that must be won at all costs in case you lose face.
Well, this time, My Lord, you have met an implaca-
ble enemy who will not be intimidated or taken by
surprise."

"You sound very sure of yourself."

"And you are not as frightening as I thought you
were."

The Earl raised his eye-brows.

"What makes you say that?"

"Because you have just reassured me, although
you may not be aware of it, that you are a gentleman and that, whatever you might do to me, you will
not hurt...Mama."

The Earl did not reply and after a moment
Thalia took a step nearer to him.

"I am right?" she questioned. "I am right about
...that?"

It was a plea and after a moment he said rue-
fully:

"I concede that, but nothing more."

He saw the relief in her eyes and it touched him.

There was something very valiant in the way she
fought for her mother.

He put down his glass of brandy and rose to his
feet.

Barbara Cartland

"I will take you home."

"Thank you," Thalia said simply.

As they went downstairs she had the feeling that she was escaping from something menacing which strangely had not frightened her as much as it should have.

The sounds of music and voices as they reached the Hall were louder than they had been before.

The Earl's carriage was waiting outside, and as they stepped into it it struck Thalia that she had just been through an experience which might at some time prove useful if she could write about it.

It would be interesting to be able to describe what a private room really looked like.

As the horses moved off, the Earl asked:

"Will you give me your hand?"

It would seem petty and childish, Thalia thought, to refuse to do what he asked.

She put out her hand towards him and he took it in both of his.

She felt the warm strength of his fingers and it gave her a rather strange sensation that she had never known before.

"Will you believe me," the Earl said in his deep voice, "if I tell you that although our dinner together was not in the least what I expected, I have enjoyed every minute we have been together, and I want more than I can tell you to see you again."

"It is too ... difficult, My Lord," Thalia replied, "and ... something we should not do."

"It is something I want to do," the Earl said, "which is a very different matter. I think, Thalia, when you go to bed tonight, it would be rather disappointing having read the first chapter of a book to find that there was no more to come and you had reached the end."

What he was saying was very reasonable and she had to admit it was true. At the same time, she was afraid.

She could not ignore him as a man, as she had been able to do for the first part of the evening, because now she was acutely conscious of his hand holding hers and that they were sitting very near to each other.

"Because I enjoy . . . talking to you, My Lord, when you are not . . . blackmailing me," Thalia said after a moment in a rather small voice, "I would like to . . . see you again, but I know it is . . . wrong and too difficult for me, so . . . please do not ask me! It would be much easier if you would just . . . disappear out of my life."

"That is something I have no intention of doing," the Earl said. "Will you believe me, Thalia, if I tell you I find you so fascinating that I shall in fact be counting the hours until I can see you again."

He saw Thalia turn her head to look at him swiftly. Then, as she was unable to see the expression on his face, she said:

"I think, My Lord, you have changed your tactics and are now . . . wooing me. I have said that I like talking to you, but it depends on what we talk about."

"I want to talk about you."

"That subject is barred and out-of-bounds."

"Then I will talk about myself."

"It depends in what connection."

The Earl gave a little laugh.

"If you are going to make all the rules, I shall have to make some too. That would only be fair, and let me add that every intelligent man and woman knows that rules are made to be broken."

As he spoke, he lifted her hand and she felt his lips first on the back of it, then he turned it over and kissed the palm.

Thalia could not think what to do or say, and as she felt the warm pressure of his mouth she quivered as something strange streaked through her whole body.

91

It was like lightning, and yet there was a pleasure, and an excitement about it which she could not describe.

She wanted to protest, she wanted to speak, but she could not find the words.

Then as she tried to take her hand from his, the horses came to a standstill and she realised that they had reached the entrance to Shepherd's Market.

The Earl set her free, and as the footman opened the door he stepped out.

Thalia knew that he was waiting for her to give him her hand so that he could help her alight, but she managed to do so without his touching her and walked quickly into the darkness of the arch leading into Shepherd's Market.

The market was quiet. There were only a very few flickering gas-lights and the stars overhead to help them find their way to Number 82, but before they reached it Thalia stopped.

"Do not come any nearer, My Lord," she said. "Hannah will be watching from the window to let me in so that Mama will not hear me."

"Then we must say good-night, Thalia," the Earl said. "When shall I see you tomorrow?"

"I have told you that is not possible."

"You know there is not such a word in my vocabulary."

"Please . . . you know I have to think . . . over what you said about . . . talking to each other . . . and it will not be . . . easy."

"Then dine with me tomorrow night."

"I . . . should not do so."

"But you will."

"I do not . . . know . . . I cannot think at this moment . . . please . . . let me think, or the decision I make might be . . . wrong."

She was pleading with him, her head thrown back because he was so much taller than she was, her eyes looking up into his.

He looked down at her, then he said quietly:

"You know that I want more than I have ever wanted anything before to kiss you good-night. Yet, because whatever you may say, I am wooing you, Thalia, gently and, as you would say, like a gentleman, I would not do anything you would not want me to do."

Thalia drew in her breath.

Something in the way he spoke, the quietness of his voice, the fact that there was no cynicism or mockery in it, made her heart beat in a very strange way.

"Thank . . . you," she said in a whisper that he could barely hear.

Then she ran away from him almost as if she would find protection and shelter waiting for her at the door of Number 82.

The Earl stood watching, noting that she did not look back at him, and wondering if she was aware how much he wanted her to do so.

Then the door opened and she disappeared inside.

* * *

Out riding the following morning before the majority of the fashonable world was awake, the Earl turned over in his mind what had happened the previous night and thought he had never spent a more interesting or intriguing two hours.

Nothing that he had expected had happened, and he knew he should be feeling frustrated and perhaps angry that his plans had gone awry.

Instead, he found himself fascinated in a manner that made him know that Thalia was different from anyone he had ever met before.

Then he told himself cynically that he was only thinking that because she had refused to accept his protection—which was something that was certainly unique in his experience.

93

He supposed that when he had decided to make her his mistress, he had not taken into account that she was decidedly of a different class from that of the women who had enjoyed his protection in the past.

"I suppose one could say she is a lady," the Earl told himself as he rode into Rotten Row.

The question was how it was possible that the term "lady," in the way it was conventionally used, could apply to a woman who was a shop-assistant and lived in a workman's house in Shepherd's Market. And who apparently had no background and no relatives with the exception of an ailing mother.

It struck the Earl that perhaps she was the love-child of some nobleman who had callously omitted to provide adequately for the baby he had fathered.

There were plenty of love-children about and often they were both beautiful and talented.

That, he thought, must be the explanation.

But those he had met in the past had always been acutely conscious of their position and certainly had not the pride or the self-possession which was, he thought, characteristic of Thalia.

She had certainly been brought up in genteel circumstances. There had been no mistakes in her behaviour at dinner last night, and the way she ate, moved, and behaved would have been acceptable at Carlton House and would have borne the scrutiny of the most critical of the great London hostesses.

She was certainly well bred, the Earl decided, and there was nothing she had done or said that he could fault.

Going over their conversation, he found that there was no other lady of his acquaintance who could equal the sharpness of her brain or the manner in which she could fence with him so that he had to use all his ingenuity not to leave her the victor.

She was well bred at least on one side of her parentage, intelligent, well educated, and yet, if Henry was to be believed, at one time she had been so impoverished that she had not enough to eat.

It was all an enigma that preoccupied the Earl's mind until several acquaintances who raised their hats to him were astonished when he rode by without even glancing in their direction.

The difficulty, he was thinking, was what he was to do about Thalia.

Her "rules" were certainly going to make it very difficult for him to see her as much as he wished to do, although he had no intention of moving out of her life as she had suggested.

It suddenly struck him that this was what he had been looking for—someone who kept him guessing, who had to be pursued as cleverly as any fox, and who would certainly make the chase an adventure such as he had never enjoyed before.

This, however, was not the reason why he had returned to London from Hellington Park, where he had decided to look for a wife.

But marriage could wait while his pursuit of Thalia could not, and he began to plan the type of house in which he would instal her, which would be very different from the one in Chelsea which had been occupied by his last mistress.

He would not insult her by putting her where he had kept any previous woman, and as he considered the houses he had seen, and what vicinity would be most suitable, he suddenly thought that perhaps after all he would not be able to persuade her to accept his proposition.

Defeat was a word which never entered the Earl's mind and in war he had always told himself that if he was not ultimately the victor, then he would die in the attempt to achieve it.

The war with Napleon was over, but he was now engaged in another campaign.

He would never give up, and yet the doubt that he might not win it was there insidiously in his mind, although he tried to shake it off impatiently.

It would be better, he thought as he rode on, if she had been shocked or shy, as he had half-expected her to be, at what he suggested because she was so young.

But that she should first of all criticise the way he had suggested that he should become her protector, and that she then should find it amusing, was yet another experience that he had not expected.

Now, because she had almost goaded him into saying he would win her, she would be suspicious of every move he made.

Because he was very experienced where women were concerned, he was aware that she had quivered when he had kissed the palm of her hand, and he thought it was the one encouraging thing about the whole evening.

And yet she had not swayed toward him as any other woman would have done when he said he wanted to kiss her.

That she had run away meant that perhaps she was not only running away from him but from herself.

The trouble was that he did not know with any certainty the answer to any of his own questions.

What did she feel about him?

When she was alone, did she really feel shocked, perhaps disgusted, because he wished her to be his mistress?

If she was the lady she appeared to be, that was understandable, but surely she must have known other men who had complimented her and perhaps, because she was so lovely, had attempted if not to seduce her at least to arouse her interest.

She had said that there was no-one, but was it likely that a girl in her position would admit to anything?

And yet she appeared to be truthful. Except that she would tell him nothing about herself, the Earl was certain that she had not lied to him.

He had learnt to recognise liars almost before they opened their mouths. He had known that strong men trembled when he asked to see them in his tent or, more usually, in some dirty peasant's house that had been commandeered for the few nights they had rested somewhere on their advance into France.

A soldier would always try to lie his way out of having looted or having raped some wretched woman. But the Earl, while he forced himself to listen to what the man had to say, knew instinctively whether or not he told the truth.

Thalia did not lie, he would stake his life on that.

He rode back towards Berkeley Square, and as he passed Shepherd's Market, deliberately riding down Curzon Street so that he could do so, he had an almost insane desire to go look at the house where she lived, as if it might tell him something about her.

Perhaps he would see her setting off for work, escorted by Hannah in the same way as she was taken home in the evening, to guard her from being molested by gentlemen like himself.

Then he told himself that to do this not only would embarrass her but he would gain nothing by it.

He had already planned that he would send a groom, preferably Henry because he was discreet, to the shop with a letter saying that he would be waiting for her tonight at the same time and at the same place.

Henry would bring back an answer, and he knew, at least he was almost sure he knew, what Thalia's reply would be.

He had a sudden vision of her dressed as he intended to dress her in the most expensive and beautiful gowns that could be purchased in London.

He would give her jewellery too, not the flashy, gaudy pieces which most of the "Fashionable Impures" thought embellished their appearance, but the very best gems like those in the Hellington collection, which had been in the Bank since his mother died and must remain there until they were required for his wife.

'That will be many years ahead,' the Earl thought. 'If I have Thalia, I shall certainly not have any time to spend looking for a wife.'

He thought how much he would like to take her to Hellington Park and show her the house which was his home and which he loved perhaps more than anything else in his life.

There was so much which he would like her to see and to which he would like to watch her reaction—so much which he knew would interest her.

There was no reason why she should not go there. After all, most of his friends had what were called "Bachelor Parties," but the guests included attractive young women who needed no Chaperone and who certainly made the evenings after they had been hunting or shooting amusing.

But that was not the sort of party he wanted to give for Thalia.

The answer to that was that he wanted her alone, not in some "private room" but seated at his dining-table in Berkeley Square, or in the great Banqueting-Hall at Hellington, which, designed by Adam, was one of the finest Dining-Rooms to be found anywhere in the country.

'I wonder what we would talk about,' he thought with a smile.

Then he remembered that even if he invited her to Hellington Park, she would almost certainly refuse the invitation. It was as if the thought was like a dash of cold water in his face.

"Damn the girl! She is more trouble than she is worth!" he told himself angrily as he reached Berkeley Square.

But he knew, even as he spoke the words beneath his breath, that he lied and that he would never give up until he had won her as he intended to do.

Chapter Five

The Earl opened the note which Henry had brought back to him and read it with a rueful expression on his face.

It was, he thought, what he might have expected, and yet he had been optimistic because never in the past had any woman in whom he had shown an interest turned him down.

But the note he held in his hand was very explicit and he read it again.

> I regret, My Lord, it is impossible for me to meet Your Lordship tonight as you suggest. I thank you for a very interesting evening.
>
> I remain, My Lord,
> Yours sincerely,
> Thalia Carver

The writing, he thought, was what he had expected—elegant, educated, and with a distinct personality about it.

He realised that the servant who had brought him the note, after Henry had returned with it to his house, was waiting.

"That will be all," the Earl said.

When he was alone, carrying the note in his hand

he walked across the room to the window to look out at the garden in the centre of Berkeley Square.

However, he did not see the trees or the flowers but only Thalia's lovely face with her wide eyes, her two irrepressible dimples, and her firm little chin.

He wondered what he could do to persuade her to dine with him.

He had the very unpleasant feeling that she had decided that they should not see each other again, and he was at a loss as to how he could break down that decision and force her to do as he wished.

He walked from the window across the room and back again.

Was it possible that after all these years of getting his own way too easily where women were concerned, he had found the one woman who was not interested in him as a man?

Then he remembered the little quiver that had passed through Thalia when he had kissed her hand, and he knew that she was interested even if it was only slightly, and perhaps that more than anything else was the reason why she was determined to have nothing to do with him.

"What shall I do?" he asked himself.

He found himself thinking of what should be his next approach almost as if in fact, as she had said, it was a battle between them.

The door opened and Richard, without being announced, came into the room.

"What are you up to, Vargus?" he asked. "I have been waiting for you at the Club."

"I am sorry, Richard," the Earl replied. "I had actually forgotten that we were to have luncheon together."

Richard looked at him sharply.

"Forgotten?" he repeated. "What is on your mind, Vargus? It is unlike you to be forgetful."

That was indeed the truth, for the Earl was extremely punctilious and Richard knew that for him to forget an engagement must mean that he was deeply preoccupied.

"You must forgive me," the Earl said quickly, as if he had no wish for Richard to search for an explanation. "As a matter of fact I have not yet eaten, and we can go to the Club or have luncheon here, whichever you prefer."

"Let us eat here," Richard said, "because I have something extremely interesting to tell you, something which will astound you, and I want your advice as to whether I shall tell the others or keep it to ourselves."

As he was talking, the Earl had rung the bell. When the door opened, he said to the Butler:

"Mr. Rowlands and I will be having luncheon here. Ask the Chef to have something ready as soon as possible."

"Very good, My Lord."

As soon as the door closed, Richard went on excitedly:

"I will give you three guesses what I have discovered."

"Why not just tell me?"

"You do not seem particularly interested."

"I am—of course I am," the Earl answered, forcing himself to concentrate on what his friend was saying.

"Then be prepared for a surprise," Richard said, and added triumphantly, "I have discovered the identity of the 'Person of Quality'!"

It took the Earl a second to remember what he was speaking about. Then he recalled the book which had both amused and annoyed the Members of White's the last time he had been at the Club.

"How could you do that?" he asked, as he knew Richard was waiting for his reaction. "And who is it?"

"A woman," Richard replied.

The Earl raised his eye-brows.

"That is certainly a surprise! At least the Members of the Club are off the hook."

"Some will be relieved, some merely annoyed," Richard replied. "Sefton was screaming only yesterday when he found one maxim which he was certain referred to him, and Toby considered himself insulted by another."

"It is obvious that they think themselves to be of more consequence than they are," the Earl said drily, "unless, of course, the author knows them and is deliberately putting their idiosyncracies in print."

"I do not know her," Richard said. "In fact I never heard of her until I discovered who the 'Person of Quality' was."

"How did you do that?" the Earl asked, forcing himself to sound attentive.

"Everyone was making such a commotion about the book that I thought I would go along to see Hatchard and find out what he had to say. After all, he published it."

"It seems quite a simple solution to the mystery," the Earl said with a smile.

"It was not as easy as that," Richard explained. "Hatchard himself refused to tell me anything. In fact I thought he was delighted to hear that people were inerested in the identity of the 'Person of Quality.'

" 'The book is selling well, Mr. Rowlands,' he said, 'so, as far as I am concerned, the more curious everyone is as to who is the author, the better!'

"I argued with him but he would not listen, and, having talked to one or two of the people I knew in the shop, I walked back into Piccadilly."

Richard paused to make sure that he held the Earl's attention, then continued:

"I had only proceeded a few paces towards St. James's Street when a man sidled up to me and said:

" 'I heard you talking to Mr. Hatchard, Sir, and saying you wanted to know who wrote the book called *Gentlemen.*'

" 'You mean you know who it is?' I asked in surprise.

"Then I saw that he was in his shirt-sleeves and wearing a large holland apron, and I guessed he was a packer or something of that sort from the shop.

" 'Are you prepared to tell me what I want to know?' I asked.

" 'Times are hard, Sir, and I've a sickly wife and three children.' "

"So he was ready to sell the information," the Earl remarked.

"I hesitated as to whether I should tell him he should be loyal to his employer or pay him to find out what I wanted to know."

"I need not ask the choice you made."

"I must admit I was too curious to resist the temptation. It cost me two guineas, but I think it was well worth it."

"What did he say?" the Earl enquired.

"He told me that the 'Person of Quality' was a woman and he had seen her when she brought the manuscript to Mr. Hatchard.

" 'A pretty piece she were, Sir,' he said, 'all dressed in grey, and I hears the Guv'nor call her Miss Carver.' "

The Earl had already stiffened when Richard had mentioned what Thalia was wearing. Now he stared at his friend incredulously before he asked:

"You are quite certain that is what the man said?"

"Quite!" Richard replied. "In fact, I made him repeat it."

"I cannot believe it!" the Earl said beneath his breath.

He walked across the room to the grog-tray and poured himself a drink.

"I thought you would be surprised that it was a

woman," Richard said, "but I wonder who she can be and how she can know so much about men. I would have been prepared to wager a hundred pounds, if I had it, that every word had been written by a man, and a gentleman at that!"

The Earl did not reply. He still had his back to his friend and appeared to be busy.

Then he turned to say:

"Forgive me for one moment, Richard, before we continue with our conversation. I have a note I have to send without delay. It will not take me long."

He walked towards the writing-desk as he spoke.

* * *

Thalia, trimming a bonnet automatically but with her usual skill, found it impossible to keep her mind on anything but the Earl.

She had gone to bed thinking of him and had been a long time going to sleep, and when she had awakened it was to think of him again.

She found herself going over their conversation of the night before.

First of all, she kept remembering the note in his voice when he bade her good-night and the strange feelings he had aroused when he had kissed the palm of her hand.

Even to recall what she had felt created an echo of it within her, and she wondered how she could have lived so long without experiencing that particular feeling and why it was like no other emotion she had ever known.

'I cannot see him again . . . I cannot!' she had thought to herself as she walked with Hannah to work.

When Henry had arrived later in the morning with a letter from the Earl, she had known even before she opened it what her answer must be.

He had forced her into dining with him last night —"blackmailed" was the right word—but it must not happen again, and she was sure, because she could appeal to his finer instincts, that in revenge he would not do anything to hurt her mother.

That was all that mattered.

At the same time, having sent Henry away with a note that she had written hastily at the desk where Mrs. Burton did her accounts, she had told herself despairingly that the conversation that had taken place the night before between herself and the Earl would be the last intelligent one in which she was likely to participate until her father's return to England.

Being with the Earl had made her realise that for the last three years her brain had been starved just as her body had been, only to a greater degree.

Sir Denzil had played such a large part in Thalia's life that when he was gone she realised what a huge void he had left and how desperately she missed him.

She loved him because he was her father, but his place as a companion had, she thought, looking back, made it an almost unique relationship between a father and daughter.

Because their minds were attuned and Thalia was so advanced for her age, they had talked as though they were equals, and Sir Denzil had found in his daughter the only thing that was lacking in the perfection of his wife, whom he adored.

Thalia thought that last night, despite the many emotions that had been evoked within her, had been an intellectual delight that she would never know again.

"It is too ... dangerous ... and I cannot go on ... deceiving Mama," she told herself.

At the same time, she knew there was a deeper reason for her decision and one that she did not wish to express in words even to herself.

The morning passed slowly. Thalia waited on two customers who as usual bought more bonnets than they had intended, and Mrs. Burton smiled at her approvingly as she returned to the work-room.

She continued with the trimming of a bonnet on which she had been engaged before she was called to the front of the shop.

"Ye've used up all th' roses, Thalia!" one of the work-girls exclaimed.

Thalia was suddenly aware that she had in fact over-decorated the bonnet to the point of absurdity.

It was pretty and at the same time sensationally theatrical. It could only have been worn by someone like Genevieve or perhaps Lady Adelaide.

"It is too much," she admitted.

She was aware that she had been working with her fingers but using her mind in a very different way.

"Pretty, though," the work-girl said. "Why don't you put it in th' window? Bet it's snapped up so quick yer'll be sitting here half the night making 'nother."

Perhaps it would be better to do that, Thalia thought, than to go home and think where she might have been instead of alone in bed with a book.

She had actually risen to take the bonnet and put it in the window, as had been suggested, when there was a knock on the back-door and one of the young matchers, who opened it, said:

"Another note for yer, Thalia! Yer're certainly a success today."

All the work-women looked at Thalia curiously.

Ever since she had been at Mrs. Burton's she had never received, as far as they knew, any attention from the outside world. Now there had been two notes in the same morning, which set everyone whispering to one another as she opened it.

It was written in the Earl's forceful hand on his crested parchment paper.

I have discovered your secret. It is something we must discuss. I shall therefore expect you to dine with me.

Hellington

Thalia stared down at what she had read almost as if she was turned to stone.

It could not be true. How could he have found out? And if he knew—who else?

She felt a sudden terror of what this might mean at this particular moment. She would have to give up her work at Mrs. Burton's and take her mother somewhere else.

They would have to find another house and perhaps change their name again, in which case when her father returned there would be another alteration to the address and he might be unable to find them.

She felt for the moment as if the ceiling had caved in and hit her on the head. Then with her usual practical common sense she thought that even if the Earl had discovered who she was, that might not mean that many other people knew.

She could persuade him, of course she could persuade him, to keep her secret to himself.

Because for the moment she was so agitated, she could not think clearly and she knew only that the Earl was right. They must discuss it and she must plead with him not to say anything, so that perhaps she would not have to take her mother away.

When she had read what he had written, she felt that her heart had stopped beating, but now she felt as it was functioning again more normally and she forced herself to walk slowly to the back-door to where Henry was waiting.

"Please . . . carry a message to your Master," she said, remembering not to mention the Earl's name.

He doffed his cap respectfully and she realised that the Earl with his usual consideration had sent his groom dressed in ordinary clothes and not wearing the Hellington livery.

"Just tell him . . . I agree," Thalia finished.

"Very good, Miss."

Thalia shut the door on him quickly, hoping

108

that the work-girls had not overheard what she had said as she had spoken in so low a voice. At the same time, she knew that if they had, they would have learnt little.

She felt weak about the knees as she walked back to her usual seat at the work-table, feeling as if the world were whirling round her and it was impossible to know how she could stop it.

*　*　*

That evening, as she helped her mother to bed, tidied the room, pulled the curtains, and finally blew out the candles, Thalia thought that it had been the longest day she had ever spent in the whole of her life.

She had see-sawed between believing that the Earl would help her by keeping silent, and planning what to do if he would not.

When her father had been forced into exile he had not realised how humiliated his wife and daughter would be.

They had not only to keep what had actually happened secret, but they had to make plausible explanations for his absence.

When Lady Caversham discovered that it was first believed he had run away from his creditors, then later from far more heinous crimes, she had not only been affronted that such aspersions should be cast on her beloved husband but also ashamed that they should have to lie on his behalf and of course on their own.

It was, Thalia realised, the only thing possible, to disappear from the County where they were so well known and certainly from their fashionable, pleasure-seeking friends in London.

She thought there were some who would have stood by them in trouble, but she was too young to know who they were and she was aware that for her mother to be snubbed by any of those who had entertained her in the past would be intolerable.

When finally she had realised that she would have to exist on the proverbial "shoe-string" until her father's return, she had thought that the best hiding-place was London because their neighbours would not be interested in them and it was always easier to be anonymous amongst a crowd.

As the years passed, she had grown used to living in the present, just has her mother lived only for the future when her husband would return.

There was no point in looking back into the past. To Thalia, because she was young, it seemed to recede month by month until she seldom thought of the days when they had been able to enjoy the luxury of carriages, servants, and the freedom of being in the country.

She felt that the only thing she had to fight was her mother's weakness and her ever-increasing fear that she might never see her husband again.

Thalia grew used to telling herself day after day that her mother must not be upset, must not be perturbed, must not lose faith.

And she knew now that the upheaval of moving house again and the fear of disclosure would injure her to the point where she might relinquish her always precarious hold on life.

'I must make the Earl understand,' Thalia kept thinking.

When finally her mother was settled for the night, she hurried into her own bedroom to change hastily into the gown she had worn the evening before, and, throwing the velvet cloak over her shoulders, she tip-toed down the stairs to the kitchen.

"You are playing with fire, that's what you are doing!" Hannah said uncompromisingly from the other side of the kitchen-table.

"I have to see His Lordship," Thalia said. "I refused to dine with him again, but then I learnt something that makes it imperative that I should ... talk to him."

There was a note of desperation in her voice that made Hannah ask sharply:

"What's he been saying to upset you?"

"I will tell you about it tomorrow," Thalia replied. "There is no time now. Oh, Hannah, when you say your prayers tonight, pray that he will do what I ask of him."

"If my prayers had been heard," Hannah said tartly, "he would not have been coming here in the first place."

"Good-night, Hannah."

Now as she turned to leave the kitchen the old maid gave a little cry.

"Have you got your pistol with you?"

"I have forgotten it, but I will not need it," Thalia answered.

"How can you be sure of that?" Hannah asked.

"I am not quite certain why, but I am."

Then without waiting for Hannah to open the front-door for her, she sped towards it, knowing that if she left it open Hannah would close it quietly behind her so that it would not disturb her mother.

The Earl was waiting in the same place as he had been the night before, and as Thalia ran towards him she had the strange feeling that, in a way she could not explain, he stood not for disruption resulting from the discovery she feared but for security.

She reached him and he took her hand in his.

"You are cold," he said.

"I am ... frightened."

"Of me?"

"No, of what you are going to tell me. How ... could you have ... found out?"

"Shall we talk about it over dinner?" he suggested.

Thalia wanted to reply that she could not wait until dinner-time to know the worst, but after the anxiety of waiting all day for this moment, now that he was here, the urgency did not seem quite so intense.

They walked to where the Earl's carriage was waiting and as they drove away the Earl said:

"Let me look at you. You are even lovelier than I remember, and I have been thinking about you ever since we said good-night."

Thalia forced a wry little smile to her lips but she had no ready reply.

He had again taken her hand in his, but he did not kiss it as she half-expected he would, but instead held it close so that she could feel the warmth coming back into it.

At the same time, she felt as if, in some way which she did not understand, she was drawing on his strength and absorbing it into herself.

The carriage came to a standstill and she looked out in surprise.

It had only been a few minutes since they had left Shepherd's Market.

"Tonight I thought we would dine at my house," the Earl said. "There are a number of things in it which I would like to show you, and I realise that where we went last night is not the right place for you."

Thalia stepped out and followed him, feeling, as she entered the large Hall with its beautiful wrought-iron staircase twisting upwards to a painted dome, that she had stepped into another world.

The Butler opened the door of the Salon and Thalia thought it was exactly the type of room she had imagined the Earl would possess.

It was decorated sumptuously but at the same time in a manner which made it appear to achieve a perfection of design and furnishing that was like listening to great music or seeing a picture painted by a great master.

But for the moment she had no interest in anything but what the Earl had to tell her, and, having accepted the glass of champagne she was proferred without even realising what she was doing, she waited until the servants left the room before she said:

"Tell me . . . tell me what you have discovered . . . and how."

"I should like you to have trusted me with your secret," the Earl said.

"How could I," Thalia replied, "when I was not the only person involved?"

"You mean somebody helped you?"

"Helped me?"

"Was it a man?"

The Earl's voice was sharp, and as Thalia looked at him in surprise, not understanding what he was saying, he said:

"I suppose I might have guessed that it could not be entirely the work of a woman. After all, only a man could have managed to put the innuendoes in such a way that each gentleman who read it would think it was referring to himself."

"Read . . . it?" Thalia said beneath her breath.

Then in a voice that was very different from the one in which she had spoken before, she said:

"Y-you . . . are talking about . . . my book!"

"Of course," the Earl replied. "What else did you think I was speaking of?"

He saw the look of relief spread over her face and bring the colour back to her cheeks and the light to her eyes.

Then she made a little sound that was half a laugh and half a sob and put her glass down on the table as if it was too heavy for her to hold.

"My . . . book, of course . . . that is what you have discovered about me!"

"I cannot actually claim the credit," the Earl said. "It was a friend of mine, who found a man in Hatchard's employment who was prepared to sell him the truth in exchange for two guineas."

"Why should he be interested?"

There was now a touch of Thalia's old spirit not only in her voice but in the look in her eyes.

The Earl laughed.

"You are obviously not aware that you have set the whole of White's by the ears. They suspected it was one of their Members who was holding them up to ridicule, and they were determined that when they discovered who he was, he should be expelled from the Club."

"You mean . . . they were . . . annoyed?"

"Quite a number of them were very annoyed."

"How many copies do you think they have bought?"

There was no doubt that she was eager to know, but the Earl had not missed the transformation that had taken place since she had discovered that it was her book he was talking about and not something which to her was infinitely more sinister.

'What can she be hiding?' he thought. 'What crime could she have possibly committed?'

Then he remembered she had said that her secret involved other people besides herself.

If it was not her mother who was in trouble, it could only be her father.

The Earl turned over in his mind how he could broach the subject. At the same time, he had no wish to frighten Thalia as she had been frightened when she had met him earlier that evening.

He could still feel the coldness of her hand when he had touched it and the way her fingers had trembled beneath his.

"Drink a little more champagne," he said. "I think you need it."

Thalia obeyed him. At the same time, she felt such a surge of relief sweeping over her that she had no need of champagne, and after the anxiety and misery of the day it was if she were suddenly enveloped in sunshine.

"Tell me about your book," the Earl said.

"Who else knows that I am the ... author of it?" Thalia asked.

"Only my friend Richard Rowlands," the Earl replied, "who discovered your identity."

"Please ... can he be ... persuaded not to tell ... anybody else?"

"I am sure he will do that if I ask him to. But, as you can imagine, he is longing to confront the Members of White's with the information that they have been made to look fools by a mere woman."

"I ... did not intend them to feel ... like that," Thalia said. "It was just when the idea came to me I remembered some of the things I had read and I suppose heard, and I ... jotted them down."

"And used your clever little brain to invent a number of others," the Earl said with a smile.

"Yes ... that is true, but if it sells a lot of copies ... then I shall make some money ... and perhaps be able to write another book."

"On the same subject?" the Earl asked. "How can you be so knowledgeable about men when you tell me you know none?"

"Mama asked me the same thing," Thalia replied. "I think the answer is that people are kind enough to find more in what I have said than what I meant in the first place."

"Now you are being modest," the Earl remarked. "You know as well as I do that your book is both witty and provocative, and, uncomfortably for some people, it hits the nail on the head!"

"Perhaps the Dandies will feel like that."

"If they do, it serves them right," the Earl answered. "They deserve everything that is said about them."

"You do not consider yourself to be a Dandy?" she asked provocatively.

"I do not!" the Earl replied firmly. "And if you
115

call me one, I shall prove very forcefully that I am a very different type of character entirely!"

Thalia laughed and it swept the last vestige of anxiety and fear from her face.

"Now you are offering me a challenge," she said. "Be careful in case I find it irresistible!"

"There are so many challenges between us," the Earl said, "the most important still being what I am to do about you."

"The answer to that is ... nothing, and that is why I refused your invitation in the first place."

"I am aware of that," he said, "but Fate in the shape of Richard Rowlands stepped in on my side and you are here."

He paused before he added very quietly:

"And that is all that matters for the moment."

They dined in the oval Dining-Room, where the polished table, clothless in the fashion set by the Regent and decorated with gold candelabra and magnificent gold plate, was to Thalia as fascinating as if she were watching a performance at Covent Garden.

The servants moved silently, dressed in their livery coats with crested buttons, serving them exotic dishes on what she knew was extremely rare and beautiful Sèvres china.

To Thalia it was an enchantment that until now had existed only in her books of fairy-stories, but she knew that the centrepiece of what was almost a pageant being unfurled before her eyes was the Earl himself.

If last night he had seemed imposing in the private room where they had dined, tonight, sitting against the crimson velvet background of his chair at the top of the table, he was magnificent.

His cravat was tied in an intricate design she had never seen before, and as his eyes searched her face in the light of the candles she felt as if she were playing the leading role in a drama.

They talked not exactly as they had done the night before, because there were often pauses in the conversation, yet, although they were silent, it was as if they were still communicating without words.

Thalia felt a strange excitement and also a shyness for which she did not understand the reason.

She told herself that it was because she had never before been in such grand surroundings or alone with a man who was so splendid in his appearance.

As soon as the dinner was over they left the Dining-Room, the Earl walking beside her towards the Salon, and she said:

"I would like to look at your treasures."

"That, before you arrived, was what I wanted you to do," he answered. "I wished to see if you appreciated them, but now they are unimportant beside you."

"You are . . . flattering me."

"I am speaking the truth."

As they walked into the Salon and she seated herself on the sofa, he said, looking down at her:

"I keep wondering what you have done to me. Ever since I have known you I find it hard to think of anything but you. When I went riding this morning, I felt that you were riding beside me, and when I came back to find your note saying that you would not meet me this evening, I felt an emotion I have never encountered before. It was one of despair."

The way he spoke made it impossible for Thalia to answer him lightly.

For a moment she did not speak. Then she said:

"I think what you are feeling is simply irritation because, having been . . . spoilt all your life, for once you are . . . unable to have your own . . . way."

"Why should you think me spoilt?" the Earl asked aggressively.

"How can you be anything else?" she replied. "Look at this house, the things you possess, and of course . . . yourself."

"Tell me about myself."

He spoke almost as if he were a child eager for praise.

"What can I say about the Earl of Hellington?" she asked. "He is a noted sportsman, he is at the top of the social pinnacle of fame, he is handsome, and he is wealthy! There must be a snag somewhere, but I have not yet found it."

"The snag is," the Earl said, "that I cannot persuade one small, extremely determined young woman to give me her heart."

"If I did," Thalia asked, "what would you do with it? Add it to all the others you have accumulated? You must have quite a valuable collection by now."

"You are not to speak to me like that," the Earl retorted.

"Why not? And because you are angry, I have the feeling that I have touched you on a raw nerve, which doubtless is the truth!"

"If there was ever an infuriating, irritating young woman, it is you!" the Earl exclaimed. "Stop jeering at me and talk to me sensibly for a change."

"If by sensibly you mean you are going to persuade me to do what I have no intention of doing now or ever, then you can save your breath!"

Thalia rose from the sofa on which she had been sitting.

"I intend to look now at all the lovely things you have in this room."

She walked resolutely towards one painting.

"A Rubens!" she exclaimed. "If you only knew how much I have always wanted to see one. The colours are superb! Just as I thought they would be. In a book I once read it said that he always painted his second wife, whom he adored, into each of his pictures."

"I have no wish to put you in a picture," the Earl said. "I want you in my arms."

Thalia turned from her contemplation of the Rubens.

"That is a very banal statement," she said, "and not really worthy of you."

"Damn you!" the Earl exclaimed. "One day you will make me lose my temper, and then there will be no use your complaining of the consequences!"

Thalia laughed.

"You do not frighten me," she said. "And now that I know what you are really like, I will let you into another secret. Last night Hannah made me bring a pistol with me when I dined with you."

"A pistol?"

There was no doubting the Earl's astonishment.

"I carried it in my satin bag. It was a very small pistol, but it could still do a lot of damage."

"Is that why you were not afraid when I said I might keep you by force?"

"Actually I doubted from the very beginning that you would behave in such a manner. The truth is, as I said last night, you are too much of a gentleman!"

"You certainly make me feel that it is a severe handicap."

"I would prefer you to think of it as a state of mind of which you can be justly proud."

"I shall not feel that if it prevents me from getting my own way."

The Earl took a step nearer to Thalia as he said:

"Let us stop fencing. I want you, Thalia, and at the moment I cannot contemplate my life without you."

There was a note in his voice which she had found difficult to resist last night, and although he had not touched her, she put out her hands as if to protect herself.

"Please . . . please," she said. "I do not want you to talk to me like this. I prefer it when we are arguing and confronting each other."

"I have no wish to confront you," the Earl said. "All I want is for you to be mine."

He saw what he thought was a little quiver go through her, and he went on:

"I think you know already, even though you will not admit it, that we mean something to each other; something which neither of us can dismiss lightly or lose without suffering in consequence."

Thalia was again studying the Rubens, and the Earl said softly:

"Look at me, Thalia."

She shook her head.

"I must go home. You know I cannot stay long."

"Not if I ask you to do so?"

"You know the answer to that."

"That is not really an answer. You are just relying on the rules you made yourself, which have no real sense where we are concerned."

"Nevertheless, they are what you have to obey."

"Why?"

"Because . . ." Thalia began, then stopped. "Please . . . take me home."

"I desperately want you to stay. Does that mean nothing to you?"

Again there was that note of appeal which she found very difficult to resist.

"Please . . ." she said.

Now she raised her eyes to his and was lost.

They gazed at each other without moving, and it seemed to Thalia that the whole world had vanished into two steel-grey eyes and there was nothing else.

They filled her heart, her body, and were part of the very air she breathed.

She was never certain afterwards whether she moved or the Earl did.

She only knew that without thought, almost unconsciously, she was in his arms and he was holding her against him.

She did not even think that she ought to struggle. It was as if her mind would no longer work, and there were only his eyes, then his lips, and as they held hers captive there was only he.

She felt that his mouth took possession of her and she was no longer herself, and it was almost as if her body melted into his and they became one person which they had been once long ago at the beginning of time.

His arms tightened and his lips became more insistent, demanding, and she felt that strange streak that was both pleasure and pain flash through her, moving from her lips to her breasts until she knew it touched her heart and again it became part of his heart and there was no escape.

She knew that what she was feeling was love; love not as she had imagined it would be but far more poignant, more wonderful, and more glorious.

It was not a question of fighting against anything, because she now belonged to him and she was no longer herself but his.

She felt as if he annihilated and captured completely the last semblance of herself alone.

This was the mystery of love, the wonder to which she could only surrender completely and absolutely.

Then at last, when she felt as if she were no longer human but part of the divine, the Earl raised his head.

"My darling, my sweet! How can you fight against this?" he asked. "You are mine—mine as you were always meant to be."

It was then that Thalia came back to reality, as if she fell from the sky down to the roughness of the earth beneath.

"Please . . ." she whispered.

As if he knew what she was feeling, he said:

"I will take you home. We will talk about what

121

we shall do tomorrow. It is late now and you are very tired."

With his arm round her, he drew her across the Salon and into the Hall.

The footman on duty hurried to fetch her cloak and when the front-door was open she saw the Earl's carriage waiting outside.

She stepped into it, too bemused for the moment even to think, and, as if he understood what she was feeling, the Earl put his arm round her and her head turned naturally against his shoulder, but he merely pressed his lips against her forehead.

They drove in silence towards Shepherd's Market. Then as they walked through the quiet streets towards Number 82, the Earl said:

"Do not worry about anything. Leave everything to me. When we meet tomorrow night, I shall have a plan for you which will make everything easy, and you will never have to worry again."

He stopped at the same place where they had parted the night before, and the Earl looked down at her.

"Good-night, my precious darling," he said tenderly. "I shall be thinking of you. Just trust me, that is all you have to do."

Thalia looked up at him.

She could see his eyes and she felt as if she was still held captive by them.

Then because her voice had died in her throat she turned and walked away from him towards the house.

Only as she waited for Hannah to open the door did she look back.

The Earl was standing where she had left him, and she felt as if he grew taller and taller until his head touched the stars.

Chapter Six

"Are yer all right, Thalia?"

The voice broke in on Thalia's thoughts and she turned to look down at the young matcher who was staring at her in surprise.

"I am sorry," she said. "Did you speak to me?"

"I've asked yer three times if yer think this velvet's what yer want for Lady Standish's bonnet."

With an effort Thalia forced herself to look at the piece of material the matcher held up in her hand.

"Yes, I think that will do very well. Thank you, Emily."

The matcher walked away and Thalia tried to remember that she must work and think of what she was doing.

It was difficult as ever since she had awakened this morning she had felt as if her heart was singing and she had been carried into a world where nothing seemed real and everything was dazzling with sunshine.

"This is love," she had told herself, "and everything is different. Nothing is the same as it was before."

Then some critical part of her mind asked her if love, to the Earl, meant the same thing as it did to her.

Because she was afraid of the answer, she could not risk depressing herself by being introspective.

The fact that she loved him presented a whole number of new problems—problems that sooner or later would have to be faced—but, just for the moment, the dazzling glory of it was all that mattered.

She had gone to bed feeling as if his kiss had carried her up to the stars and left her there suspended high above the earth where nothing frightening could encroach upon her.

"Now I have to face reality," she told herself severely.

She picked up the bonnet on which she was working and tried to remember how she had intended to decorate it and who it was for.

Just as she was starting to thread her needle, Mrs. Burton came hurrying from the front of the shop.

"Lord Dervish is here," she whispered, "with that tiresome sister of his, Lady Wentmore. Don't forget to put ten percent on his bill so that he can take it off."

This would have been an incomprehensible instruction to anyone outside the shop, but Thalia knew exactly what Mrs. Burton meant.

There were a certain number of her clients who argued about the price of everything they bought and insisted on a reduction. Of those, Mrs. Burton always asked more to begin with than she expected to obtain.

There were also those like Lord Dervish, who automatically cut ten percent off the bill when he paid it.

The same adjustment to the price therefore applied to him.

Without hurrying, Thalia walked gracefully into the front of the shop to find, as she had anticipated, that Mrs. Burton was serving a petulant, temperamental beauty who was determined to try on every bonnet available before she decided which one she would buy.

In front of another mirror Lord Dervish and his sister were waiting.

Thalia curtseyed respectfully.

"Good-morning, My Lady," she said to Lady Wentmore, whom she had served on several other occasions.

Her Ladyship wasted no time in the courtesies.

"I want to see your prettiest and newest bonnets and those that are most original," she said sharply, "and I shall be extremely annoyed if I see anyone in a replica of what I am wearing myself."

"You will not do that, My Lady," Thalia promised. "We pride ourselves on never turning out the same model twice."

Lady Wentmore sniffed as if she did not believe what Thalia was saying, but she sat down in front of the mirror, patting her skilfully dyed hair into place.

Fifteen years ago she had been an outstanding beauty, but now she was fading a little while striving with every known artifice to keep her looks and a semblance of youth.

Lord Dervish, who was almost a Dandy in his appearance, was obviously intent on his own thoughts and took no notice of Thalia.

"As I was telling you, my dear," he said to his sister, "I said to the Chancellor of the Exchequer: 'Things need to be tightened up. If nobody pays their taxes as they should, how can we ever expect to afford an Army, a Navy, and all the other responsibilities which have to be met?'"

"I am sure you are right," Lady Wentmore murmured.

She was turning her head from side to side to see the effect of a very attractive bonnet that Thalia had just placed on her head.

"That reminds me," Lord Dervish went on, "I had a surprise last evening."

He waited for his sister to ask what it was, and as she did not do so, he continued:

"Lawson has just returned from America, and who do you think he saw there?"

"I have no idea," Lady Wentmore murmured.

"Caversham! Denzil Caversham, strutting about, Lawson said, as if he owned the place!"

"Sir Denzil?" Lady Wentmore exclaimed. "I thought he was dead!"

"Very much alive, from what Lawson was saying," Lord Dervish answered. "And if he comes back to this country I have a surprise waiting for him."

At the mention of her father's name Thalia felt as if she was turned to stone. Then when Lord Dervish said he was alive and apparently well, her relief was so overwhelming that she felt as if it might physically sweep her off her feet.

"I am waiting to try on another bonnet!" Lady Wentmore said sharply.

Hardly realising what she was doing, Thalia picked up the nearest to her hand and placed it on Her Ladyship's head.

"You were saying you had a surprise for Sir Denzil," Lady Wentmore prompted as Thalia tied the ribbons under her chin. "What sort of surprise?"

"It is one he will not relish, nor forget in a hurry," Lord Dervish answered.

There was an unpleasant note in his voice which made Thalia hold her breath.

"Do tell me what it is, Arthur, and stop being so mysterious," Lady Wentmore said. "I always had rather a partiality for Sir Denzil. He was so attractive and danced exceedingly well."

"When he comes back to England, you will not be dancing with him for a long time," Lord Dervish replied.

"Why not?" Lady Wentmore enquired.

"Because, my dear, he will be in the Fleet!"

"In prison? What do you mean, Arthur, and why should he go to prison?"

"Because that is where I intend to send him," Lord

Dervish said. "You could hardly believe it, but the damned fellow slipped out of the country owing me one thousand pounds!"

There was no doubt that he had aroused his sister's interest, for she turned from the mirror to face him.

"One thousand pounds, Arthur? How did he come to owe you so much?"

"A debt of honour, my dear—at least it is to those who are honourable!"

"Oh, you mean cards!"

"Yes, I mean cards," Lord Dervish snapped. "Caversham gave me his IOU but I learnt it was as worthless as the paper on which it was written."

"Are you telling me that was why he went abroad?" Lady Wentmore asked.

"Mine was not the only debt he owed. I hear he was heavily indebted to his tradesmen and decided to vanish. Damned unsporting, if you ask me. No gentleman would behave in such a manner!"

"It sounds very unlike Sir Denzil to me," Lady Wentmore said, turning back to the mirror, "and doubtless when he returns he will repay you."

"I am making sure of that," Lord Dervish said, "by taking out a warrant for his arrest."

Lady Wentmore gave a little cry.

"Oh, Arthur, that would be too cruel! I cannot bear to think of someone of Sir Denzil's elegance incarcerated in that horrible debtors' prison at the Fleet. I hear the conditions there are intolerable!"

"It will teach him a lesson," Lord Dervish said with satisfaction, "and personally, I never cared for the fellow myself, despite the fact that you and your friends fluttered round him like a lot of stupid moths round a candle!"

He paused to add:

"You did not get your wings burnt—I did! I intend to make him suffer, if it is the last thing I do!"

Lord Dervish spoke with a vindictive spitefulness, and Thalia, listening with a kind of sick horror, realised that the stories about his meanness and his avarice were all too true.

Mrs. Burton had always said he was the one person amongst her customers whom she dreaded seeing in the shop, knowing he would beat her down to the very last penny, then deduct his inevitable ten percent from the bill.

A thousand pounds!

For her father to owe so much to a man like Lord Dervish was as terrifying as being faced with the National Debt or the bill for the entertainment at Carlton House.

Everything that could be sold had gone from the Manor in the country, and, living only on what she earned, Thalia thought she would find it impossible to produce a thousand pennies let alone the same number of sovereigns.

Her father would receive no mercy from Lord Dervish.

At the same time, he had been seen in America. He was well and, she thought, perhaps making plans to return home now that his three-year exile was over.

She felt as if there was a conflict within her that tore her in pieces: gladness that her mother's fears that her father was dead were wrong, and horror at the idea that once he set foot on English soil, he would be arrested and taken to the Fleet.

Lady Wentmore was not the only person who had heard of the terrors of the prison where men who could not pay their bills languished amongst the criminals, pick-pockets, and prostitutes for years on end.

How could she contemplate her father being in such a place?

And yet she knew that Lord Dervish would make good his threat and, what was more, would enjoy humiliating a man who had not only lost to him at cards but in his opinion had deliberately defrauded him.

It was difficult for the moment to realise the full horror of what she had just heard, but of one thing she was quite certain—that if, as Lord Dervish intended, her father was arrested the moment he arrived, it would kill her mother.

She would not be able to stand the shock and the humiliation after what she had suffered already.

'I must do something! I must do something immediately!' Thalia thought frantically.

Vaguely, as if from the end of a very long tunnel, she heard Lady Wentmore say:

"I will take the blue bonnet. I think I look better in that than in any of the others. Do you not agree, Arthur?"

"Yes, the blue suits you admirably, my dear."

"And it was very sweet of you to say you would give it to me as a present," Lady Wentmore said. "Thank you very much."

"Wait a minute! Wait a minute!" Lord Dervish cautioned. "You are going too fast! I have to find out the price. I do not intend to be taken for a greenhorn."

Lady Wentmore laughed a tinkling little laugh that somebody had once told her sounded like bells.

"Nobody would ever suspect you of being a greenhorn, Arthur! You are far too astute, far too clever in every way."

"I hope so," Lord Dervish said complacently.

Thalia looked across the shop to Mrs. Burton, who, seeing that Lady Wentmore had replaced her own bonnet, made her excuse to her client and came to Lord Dervish's side.

"I understand Her Ladyship is satisfied," she said, "and I hope you are too, My Lord. As an old and valued customer, we always do our best to give you satisfaction."

"That depends on one thing and one thing only," Lord Dervish began.

Carrying the blue bonnet in her hand, Thalia escaped to the back of the shop.

"Pack this up," she said to one of the work-women, "and tell Mrs. Burton, if she asks where I am, that I have just gone out for a breath of air."

"A breath o' air?" the work-woman repeated. "That's not like ye, Thalia. I thought ye never left th' place 'til 'twas time to go home."

Thalia did not even bother to answer. She was slipping on her grey bonnet.

Then without saying any more she opened the back-door and stepped out into the street.

She stood irresolute for one moment, then lifted her skirts in both hands and started to run.

If it was a surprise to the passers-by to see anybody running down Hay Hill into Berkeley Square, Thalia did not notice them.

Still running, swerving to avoid anybody walking in the opposite direction, she was breathless by the time she reached the imposing entrance to Hellington House.

Only then did she stop to draw in a deep breath which she hoped would ease the frantic beating of her heart.

As she did so, the front-door opened and two footmen wearing the Earl's livery came out to start laying a red carpet which would cover the steps and run out over the pavement.

A second later Thalia saw the Earl's Phaeton being driven round the corner.

She realised that she was only just in time.

She walked up the steps and as she reached the front door she saw standing in the Hall the Butler who had waited at dinner last night.

"I wish to speak to His Lordship," she said.

"Good-morning, Miss," the Butler replied politely. "I'll tell His Lordship you're here."

Thaila followed him across the Hall and he showed her into an attractive room that she thought from its appearance must be the Morning-Room or used perhaps only for callers like herself who arrived without an appointment.

But she could not think of anything except her father and the trap he would walk into the moment he arrived in England.

It seemed to her that she waited for a long time before the door opened again and the Butler said:

"Will you come this way, Miss? His Lordship's in the Library."

Feeling as if it was impossible to think of what she would say, conscious only that her mother's life as well as her father's freedom rested on what happened in the next few minutes, Thalia followed the Butler across the Hall.

He opened the door of a room where the walls were lined with books.

However, she could see only the Earl moving towards her, and with one glance at his face she was aware of his surprise at seeing her.

He waited until the door had shut behind the Butler, then he asked:

"What has happened? Why are you here?"

She raised her eyes to his and when he saw her eyes, he looked at her for a long moment before he said quietly:

"You have had a shock. Come and sit down and tell me about it."

It flashed through his mind that perhaps her mother had died. Then because of her expression he knew that something unexpectedly traumatic had happened, otherwise she would not have come to him.

The Earl had in fact been astonished when, just as he was about to leave the house, the Butler had come into the Library to say:

"There is a lady to see you, My Lord."

"A lady?" the Earl had asked sharply, thinking it might be Lady Adelaide and having no wish for her to delay his departure.

"It is the young lady who dined here last night, My Lord."

For a moment the Earl thought he could not have heard aright, then he said quickly:

"Show her in here."

"Very good, My Lord."

When the Butler left the room to fetch Thalia, the Earl told himself that something very strange indeed must have occurred for her not only to communicate with him so early in the day but to come in person.

He had been worrying ever since he awoke this morning as to whether Thalia would once again refuse to dine with him unless he could find a very reasonable excuse to force her into doing so.

Last night when he left her, she had certainly not said that she was not prepared to listen to the plan of which he had spoken or that they could not meet as he intended, but he had been afraid that when she left him she would once again be making difficulties.

Only because she was afraid of what he had discovered about her—and Heaven knows what her secret was—had she dined with him last night.

Even though he wanted to believe that the magical kiss they had exchanged had changed everything, he could not be sure of it.

Yet, inexplicably, almost unbelievably, she was here to see him and he knew without being told that it would not be just for the pleasure of his company.

Now as he looked at her, he realised how upset she was and he wanted to allay her fears and take away her unhappiness whatever the reason might be.

"I will . . . not sit down," Thalia said almost inaudibly. "There is . . .just something I want to . . . ask you . . . but it is . . . difficult to put it . . . into words."

"I can see you are upset," the Earl said, "and I think too you have been hurrying to get here. Let me send for some coffee, or perhaps it would be better for you to have a glass of wine."

"I . . . want . . . nothing, just for you to . . . listen to me."

"You know I will do that," the Earl said. "But I hate to see you like this. Give me your hand, darling."

"No . . . no!" Thalia cried. "You must not . . . touch me . . . please . . . do not . . . touch me . . . not until you have heard what I have to . . . say."

The Earl was surprised, but because it was what she wanted, he stood waiting, while he knew she was feeling for words.

It was difficult to see her face, for she bent her head and her grey bonnet obscured everything but her small, determined chin.

The Earl waited, curious and at the same time feeling that any questions he might ask would only make it more difficult.

At last it seemed that Thalia controlled herself enough to raise her eyes to his.

"You . . . asked me," she began in a very small voice, little above a whisper, "if I would be . . . your mistress."

"A harsh word," the Earl said, "for something which, where we are concerned, would be something very different, something which I believe, Thalia, would make us both very happy."

"I cannot . . . do what you . . . want . . . the way you want," Thalia said, "because Mama must . . . never know . . . but if . . ."

She stopped for a moment as if it was impossible to say any more. Then with what was a superhuman effort she went on:

"If I . . . stay with you as I could . . . have done last . . . night or the night before . . . would you give me . . . one thousand . . . p-pounds?"

The last word came out in a rush almost as if she found it impossible to say, until it burst from her lips.

Now she could no longer look at him, but he saw the burning flush that swept over her face before she bent her head.

"A thousand pounds!" the Earl said slowly.

"P-please . . ." Thalia began, "I must have it now . . . at once . . . I cannot . . . wait!"

Once again she had raised her face to his, and her eyes were searching his frantically, as if her very life depended on his answer.

"Who is blackmailing you?"

"Nobody . . . it is not . . . like that . . . it is something . . . very different."

"Will you tell me the reason why you need this money?"

"I cannot do that . . . although I want to . . . but it is a secret."

"The secret you thought I had discovered last night?"

"Y-yes."

"And as you said, it concerns someone else?"

"Y-yes."

For a moment the Earl did not speak, and Thalia said desperately:

"Please . . . do not ask questions . . . I cannot answer them. It is impossible . . . but I have to have the money . . . and if you will not give it to me . . . I do not know to whom I can . . . turn or . . . where I can . . . go."

The Earl looked down at her and now her eyes were beseeching his and he saw too that there was a terror in their depths that had not been there before, the terror of fear that he might refuse her.

"I will give you the money," the Earl said quietly.

He knew by the way Thalia drew in her breath how afraid she had been that he would not.

"I suppose," he went on, "you do not wish a cheque, because it would bear my name."

"No, no! It must be in . . . notes!"

"Very well," the Earl replied. "Just wait here."

He walked from the room as he spoke, and Thalia, as if her legs would no longer hold her, sank down in a chair and put her hands up to her face.

He would help her and her father would be safe!

For the moment she could think of nothing else, not even of what she had promised in order to obtain the money.

All that mattered was that her mother must never know, and her father could come home safely.

She realised how petrified she had been that the Earl would refuse to give her the money immediately and would say instead that she could earn it as time passed.

Had he done that, it would have been like hanging on a cliff's edge, wondering every moment of the day whether her father would arrive in England before the debt was paid, only to be arrested as he stepped off the ship.

"He will be safe now . . . safe," she told herself, and tried not to think of anything except her mother's happiness and that soon they would all be together again.

The door opened and the Earl came back into the room.

He held nothing in his hands, and for a moment, almost like the stab of a dagger, Thalia wondered if he had changed his mind and perhaps would tell her that it was impossible to give her the money after all.

Almost as if he sensed what she was feeling, he said:

"My secretary is getting what you require. Fortunately, we always keep quite a considerable sum of money here in the safe. While we are waiting, I am going to insist that you have a glass of wine."

He did not wait for her answer but went to the grog-tray which stood in a corner of the room and poured from a bottle which he took from a silver wine-cooler.

He brought the glass to her and put it in her hand.

"I do not . . . want it," Thalia said.

"But you will drink it to please me."

"Yes . . . of course."

There was a note of humility in her voice and it suddenly struck her that she had now committed herself to do what he required of her, whatever it might be.

'I am grateful . . . very, very grateful,' she thought.

At the same time, she felt as if already she had lost what she told him she prized so highly—her self-respect.

Now she would take her place with women like Genevieve, who entertained gentlemen in her nightgown and expected the man to whom she had just been introduced to pay for the pleasure of looking at her.

"I must not think of it," Thalia told herself.

Nevertheless, the thoughts were there, crowding in on her and making her feel as if she had ceased to be herself but instead was like the type of women whom she had despised even while she waited on them as a humble shop-assistant.

The Earl did not speak and neither did she.

She sipped her wine because he had ordered her to do so, aware, although she did not look up at him, that his eyes were on her face.

The door opened and the Earl's secretary came into the room.

He held a large, bulky envelope in his hand.

The Earl walked across the room towards him.

"I have included notes of the highest value we have, My Lord," the secretary said.

"Thank you," the Earl replied.

He took the package and as the door closed he reached Thalia's side and held it out to her.

"This is what you require," he said, "and because I do not think you should walk about with such a large sum of money on you, may I leave it anywhere you wish? Or may I take you there in my Phaeton?"

"Will you ... take me ... back to the shop?"

"If that is what you want," the Earl agreed.

She put down her glass and, holding the envelope in her hand, rose to her feet.

She looked at him, her eyes very wide and a little frightened in her pale face.

"I want to say ... thank you."

"Shall we leave that until this evening?" the Earl asked.

"Y-yes ... of course."

There was an apprehensive note in the words which he did not miss.

"Before we leave," the Earl said, "there is something I want to say."

Thalia looked up at him and he thought she was trembling.

"It is this," he said. "The money I have given you is a gift that has no strings attached, and I do not want your gratitude in any way that you have not shown me already."

"You mean ... ?" Thalia began incredulously.

"I mean, my darling," the Earl said, "that nothing has changed as far as I am concerned from the way it was when we left each other last night. What you have asked me for is something quite different from what we have discussed previously or intended to discuss tonight or at any other time."

As if she understood what he was saying, he saw the tears come into her eyes, making them seem larger and even more beautiful than they were before.

"How can you ... be so ... different from what I ... expected," she asked, "and so much more ... understanding?"

The tears overflowed and ran down her cheeks.

"That is another question I will answer tonight," he said, "when we have more time. I have a feeling now that you should be back at your work. I would not wish you to get into trouble on my account."

Thalia's lips quivered but she could not speak, and the Earl took his handkerchief from his breast-pocket and very gently wiped away the tears on her cheeks.

"I am sure everything will be all right," he said, "and better still if you trust me as I want you to do. I just want you to realise I am there to help you in any way I can."

"I ... love ... you!"

The words were barely audible but the Earl heard them.

"I have a lot to tell you about my love for you," he said, "but it is going to take a very long time. Now, since the Regent is waiting for me and he very much dislikes being kept waiting, I suggest we leave all the things we have to say to each other until tonight."

Thalia thought that from the expression in his eyes and the feeling, although he was no longer touching her, that she was really in his arms, there was no need for words.

She knew they were as close to each other as they had been when he had kissed her, and she was sure that he felt the same.

They walked across the room side by side and the Earl helped her into the Phaeton.

As they drove away down Berkeley Square she thought the sunshine was more golden and glittering than she had ever seen it before in her whole life.

As the horses moved a little slower up Hay Hill, the Earl asked:

"Shall I take you to the back-door?"

"Yes ... please," Thalia replied.

As she spoke, she thought it would be always the back-door in his life where she was concerned, and yet he was treating her not only as a woman he could possess but as something infinitely more precious. It reminded her of the way her father had always treated her mother.

"I love you, I love you!" she wanted to say to him over and over again.

But she remembered that the groom was sitting behind them and might hear what she said.

The Earl drew up his horses outside the back-door of the shop.

"You are quite certain I cannot help you further?" he asked.

"No . . . I am all . . . right," Thalia replied.

She put out her hand, and as he took it in his she felt herself quiver because he was touching her.

The groom helped her to step down from the Phaeton and she slipped in through the back-door, hoping that none of the work-women would be aware of the way in which she had returned.

Fortunately, when she got inside, it was to find that Mrs. Burton was still serving in the front of the shop.

It was easy for Thalia to go to the desk where the bills were made out and procure a sheet of plain paper.

On it she wrote:

The Trustees of Sir Denzil Caversham's Estate enclose the sum of £1,000 owed to Lord Dervish, and deeply regret that this sum has been overlooked and was not paid three years ago as it should have been.

She took an envelope from the desk and slipped into it the one containing the money and also the letter.

Then she folded the top of the envelope and sealed it with the sealing-wax which Mrs. Burton kept to use when money had to be taken to the Bank.

Thalia then addressed the envelope:

The Rt. Hon. Lord Dervish,
White's Club,
St. James's Street.

When she had finished, she asked:
"Is Bill here?"

139

"Yes, Thalia," one of the work-women replied. "'E's just a-going ter take this bonnet round ter Lady Wentmore. She said at first she'd take it with 'er, then 'er changed 'er mind."

"I will give it to Bill," Thalia said.

She picked up the box from the work-table and went down to the basement where Bill sat when he was not delivering packages containing the purchases the customers had made.

He was not idle, for Mrs. Burton found innumerable things to occupy him.

There were parcels and crates from Paris to be unpacked. There were things to be mended, and a great deal of his time was spent in cleaning and polishing. Mrs. Burton saw no reason to engage anyone else to do the work that he could do.

He was over forty, had grey hair, and was terrified of losing his job, and when Thalia called him he said quickly:

"Oi be comin'," as if he was half-expecting to be reproved for tardiness.

"There is a box to take to Lady Wentmore, who lives in Curzon Street, Bill," Thalia said. "And would you be very obliging and leave this letter for me at White's Club? It is not very much out of your way."

"'Twouldn't matter if it were," Bill replied. "Oi'd do anythin' to 'elp yer, Miss. Yer knows that."

"Thank you, Bill, it is very kind of you, but be careful of this envelope. It is rather valuable."

"'Ave yer ever known me to lose anythin', Miss Thalia?"

"There is always a first time, Bill."

"Not when I be a-lookin' after somethin' as belongs to yer, Miss."

"Thank you, Bill. I am very grateful."

Thalia went upstairs, thinking that Lord Dervish, with his spite and hatred for her father, would have a surprise when he found what the letter contained.

The rest of the day seemed to pass more slowly than usual except when Thalia thought of the Earl, and she found that in those moments she had no idea of time or anything else.

"How can he be so kind, so marvellous to me?" she asked herself.

And yet she told herself that perhaps it was wrong and dishonest of her to accept such overwhelming generosity and give nothing in exchange.

She was not absolutely certain what happened when a man and a woman made love to each other. She only knew that she had always believed it was wrong and wicked unless their union was blessed by the Church.

Now she could not help feeling that perhaps if the Earl made love to her it would be as wonderful as his kiss had been.

Then she was shocked at her own thoughts.

Of course it would be wrong, most of all because she would then become, as she had sworn she never would be, his mistress, whatever he might call it.

In her mother's eyes, that would be so degrading and appalling that she knew Lady Caversham must never, never learn of it.

Walking home with Hannah, Thalia knew that if she told Hannah what the Earl had suggested she should become when they first dined together, the maid would not be surprised.

It was the way she had expected a gentleman of the Earl's standing would behave with those he considered his inferiors. The only thing that would have shocked her was that his invitation was given to someone who had been born a lady and was therefore, in Hannah's eyes, his equal.

'That is something he will never consider me to be,' Thalia thought, and suddenly felt as if the sun had gone down and darkness already covered the earth.

Thinking of herself, she felt ashamed because they were nearly home before she asked Hannah:

141

"How has Mama been today?"

"Rather depressed," Hannah replied. "Her Ladyship had a little weep after luncheon when we talked about your father. She thinks perhaps he'll never come home, since it's nearly a week now since his three years were over."

"Is it really that?" Thalia asked. "I suppose I had lost count."

Then she told herself that she had good tidings for her mother. After all, she need not explain in what context she had heard it, but at least she could say that her father was alive, well, and had been seen in America.

"I have news for Mama," she said with a lilt in her voice. "She will not be depressed tonight when she hears what I have to tell her."

"News?" Hannah questioned, instinctively walking quicker.

"I must first tell it to Mama," Thalia said.

Hannah opened the door and she ran upstairs.

Lady Caversham was lying on the *chaise-longue* as usual.

"There you are, my dearest!" she exclaimed. "I have been lying here reading your book and thinking how amusing it is. I had no idea I had such a clever daughter."

"That is what I wanted you to say, Mama," Thalia answered, "and I have something to tell you, something you have been waiting to hear."

She saw the sudden alertness in her mother's eyes, then even as she opened her lips to speak, she heard Hannah's voice sounding curiously like a scream downstairs.

Lady Caversham was startled.

"What is it?" she asked.

"I will go and see," Thalia replied.

Even as she turned, she heard a man's voice answering Hannah and footsteps coming up the stairs.

For a moment she could hardly believe it was true, then she gave a cry which seemed to echo and re-echo round the room.

"It is Papa! I know it is Papa!"

"So you were expecting me," Sir Denzil said.

Then he was in the room, looking for his wife, and a second later she was in his arms.

"Papa, how could you arrive just when you are wanted most?" Thalia asked.

He could not answer her but as she kissed his cheek he put his arm round her and held her as close to him as he could.

Lady Caversham was crying helplessly against his shoulder.

"It is all right, my darling, I am back. Everything is going to be all right now, with no more worries, no more troubles. How could I have guessed, how could I have known, that you would not have enough money?"

"It does not matter," Lady Caversham sobbed, "but I thought you might be dead!"

"Dead!" Sir Denzil cried. "I am very much alive! Listen my precious, Listen, Thalia! I am rich! Immensely, enormously rich!"

Thalia moved in his arms to stare at him.

"Rich, Papa?"

"A millionaire several times over."

"But how? How is it possible?"

"It is a long story, but shall I tell you simply that I now own a Gold Mine and a very successful one at that!"

"Denzil, why did you not write to me?" Lady Caversham asked.

"Write?" Sir Denzil exclaimed. "I wrote the first month."

"I never received the letters," his wife murmured.

"Then," Sir Denzil went on, "I could hardly write, my darling, when I was living in the back of beyond!"

"And you really own a Gold Mine, Papa?" Thalia asked.

"I not only own it, but I have floated a Company on the Stock Market which will make me even richer than I am already!"

"I cannot believe it!" Thalia exclaimed.

"I will tell you all about it," he said, "but first I must tell your mother how much I love her and apologise for not letting her know sooner that I can now give her everything in the world she has ever wanted."

"All I want is ... you, Denzil," Lady Caversham murmured tearfully.

Her husband smiled over her head at his daughter in a conspiratorial fashion.

"That is what you have got," he said, "and I would have been here sooner, my darling, if I had not thought it expedient to call on Lord Eldon first."

Thalia looked at him apprehensively.

"It is all right? You are allowed to return?" she asked in a low voice.

"The Lord Chancellor was exceedingly kind," Sir Denzil replied. "He did suggest, and I think he is right, that we should leave for the country immediately and stay there until it is generally accepted that I am back and all my affairs are in order."

"That is what Mama has always planned we would do," Thalia said.

"And that is what we will do," her father replied. "I do not suppose you have much to pack? There are two carriages waiting for us."

"You intend we should leave now?"

"What is there to keep us?" Sir Denzil replied. "We will not require any of this rubbish in the future."

He waved a disparaging hand towards the furniture in the room, then he looked down at his wife with an expression of love and consternation in his eyes.

"I will make up to you, my precious, for everything you have suffered while I have been away," he promised, "and now you shall have all the things you gave up for me, diamonds, jewels, horses, and we will do all the repairs on the Manor that we always planned we would do when my 'ship' came in."

He gave a laugh with a triumphant note in it.

"Well, my ship is in and a very large one it is."

'It is like old times,' Thalia thought, to have her father boasting of his triumphs, elated by some success, and seeming to make everything he said an excitement in itself.

He bent and kissed his wife again before he said:

"Get your cloak and your bonnet, my beloved. We are leaving at once, and if we hurry we will be home in time for a late dinner."

"But, Denzil, there are no servants."

"That is where you will get a surprise," her husband said. "I went home first, expecting to find you there. Then I heard what had happened, and I told nearly everyone in the village to come and look after us until we get things organised. They will do it, you can be sure of that."

"Oh, Denzil, it does not seem true that you are here and I need be unhappy about you—no longer."

As she spoke, there was a note in Lady Caversham's voice which Thalia knew was not tiredness or lassitude but an overwhelming happiness.

It would be a long journey home, but she had a feeling it would not tire her mother half so much as sitting being miserable as she had these last three years.

The mere fact that her father was back made her mother look radiant and there was a flush on her cheeks and her eyes were shining as if she were a young woman again.

"Come along," Sir Denzil said firmly. "Hurry, Thalia. I have no intention of spending a night in this poky little hole."

They were being swept along on the flood-tide of her father's vitality, Thalia thought.

But while it was wonderful to have him there, thrilling to know he was alive and well, there was nevertheless a nagging feeling in her heart that told her his return could not be as perfect for her as it was for her mother.

'I must tell the Earl . . . I must let him know what has . . . occurred,' she thought.

Even as she thought of it she knew it was something she must not do.

If he learnt who she really was, then he would feel obliged, after all that had passed between them, to offer her marriage.

She would have caught him as he had said he had avoided being caught all these years.

She remembered only too clearly how she had told him that the women she waited on bought their clothes as a bait to catch a fish, and had laughingly added that the Earl of Hellington would be a very large catch if they could land him.

She could still hear the note in the Earl's voice as he had said:

"I assure you, I fight ferociously never to be netted!"

She had told him she spoke prophetically and that in the end he would be caught, and once he was in the net there would be no escape.

"That is exactly what I am afraid of," the Earl had said.

He had no wish to be married, that was obvious, not even to someone he loved.

"That is why," Thalia told herself as she reached for the cloak she had worn when she dined with the Earl, to put it over her thin gown, "he must never know who I really am."

Her whole being cried out in an agony at the thought of going away, of disappearing and never letting him know what had happened to her.

146

Then suddenly she remembered what had happened today.

Strangely, it was the first time it had occurred to her since her father's return that she had tried to save him from being arrested by repaying the money he owed, which the Earl had given her at luncheon-time.

His arrival had swept from her mind everything except of course her love for the Earl.

She went back into the Drawing-Room.

Hannah was there wrapping her mother in shawls so that she would not be cold on the journey.

"I want to speak to you, Papa," Thalia said.

"What is it, my dearest?" he asked. "Now that I look at you, I see you have grown extremely attractive while I have been away."

"Thank you, Papa, but this is important."

She drew him out of the Drawing-Room and into her own tiny bedroom.

"Listen, Papa, there is no time to explain now, although I will tell you later, but I need to have one thousand pounds immediately. Is that possible?"

"One thousand pounds?" her father asked. "Whatever for?"

"It is a debt of honour. Something you owed and which you forgot to pay before you left England."

"One thousand pounds?"

He put his hand up to his forehead.

"My God! It is the money I lost to Dervish!"

"Yes, I know. He has threatened to have you arrested the moment you arrive in England."

"Well, I will soon put that right," Sir Denzil said.

"I have done so already," Thalia replied, "but now that you are here, I must repay the money at once!"

"But of course," Sir Denzil agreed. "Who was kind enough to rescue me from the heavy hand of the Law?"

He spoke jokingly and Thalia answered:

"There is no time for questions, and I do not

want Mama to know what has happened. It would upset her. Can you give me the thousand pounds now?"

"If you had told me earlier, it might have been easier," Sir Denzi said. "But wait a minute! I have a Bearer Bond with me."

"Does it bear your name?" Thalia asked quickly.

"No. As a matter of fact, I called the issue after the place where I found the Gold Mine."

"Then that is all right," Thalia said, "as I do not wish the person to whom I am sending it to know who you are."

Her father looked at her with a puzzled expression on his face, then as he was about to speak, Lady Caversham called from the Drawing-Room:

"I am ready, Denzil!"

"I will be with you in a second, my dearest," he answered. "I have something to do for Thalia first."

He ran down the stairs, saying as he did so:

"Tell Hannah to get your mother into the carriage. You wait here!"

A few minutes passed, then for the second time that day Thalia put a thousand pounds into an envelope.

As she did so, she thought of something else.

She picked up one of her own books which were still lying on the dressing-table and opened it to write inside:

To a gentleman who is kind, gentle, understanding, and very, very wonderful, and whom I will never forget.

Thalia

She put it with the Bearer Bond in an envelope and addressed it to the Earl of Hellington.

As her father and Hannah tucked her mother up into the big, comfortable carriage drawn by four horses that was waiting for them on the road by the side of the market, Thalia ran to the nearest butcher-shop.

"Good-evening, Miss Carver," the butcher said. "You're later than usual!"

"I want you to do me a great favour," Thalia said. "Will you send your son, or someone trustworthy, with this letter to the Earl of Hellington in Berkeley Square?"

"Yes, of course, Miss Carver," the butcher agreed. "It'll be no trouble—no trouble at all!"

"You will ensure that it is delivered safely?"

"You need have no fears on that score. It'll be in His Lordship's hands within ten minutes o' your giving it to me."

"Thank you very much," Thalia said, "and thank you also for all your kindness to me and my mother since we have been living in the Market."

"You're leaving?"

"Yes . . . we are leaving," Thalia answered. "We are . . . going home!"

Chapter Seven

The Earl walked into the Coffee-Room at White's and threw himself down in a chair beside Richard.

One glance at his friend's face was enough to tell him that he had been unsuccessful in his search.

"Will you have a drink?" Richard enquired.

The Earl hesitated, as if it was difficult to concentrate on the question. Then he replied:

"Order me a brandy."

The waiter took the order and Richard asked in a low voice:

"No luck?"

"None at all," the Earl replied.

As he spoke, he was thinking despairingly that it was now ten days since Thalia had disappeared.

He thought he had known from the moment he received the one-thousand-pound Bearer Bond and read the inscription in her book that she was determined never to see him again.

"Whom I will never forget."

He was sure that the words were written on his heart and would haunt him all his life.

"It seems extraordinary that anybody can disappear so completely!" Richard exclaimed.

It was the same remark he had made a hundred times before, in fact, ever since the third day of his search, when the Earl had confided in him as if he

150

could not bear being alone with his anxiety any longer.

As the waiter brought the brandy to the Earl, both men were thinking of the steps they had taken to trace one elusive young woman about whom they knew so little that it had made the difficulty of finding her almost insuperable from the beginning.

Investigations by Henry in Shepherd's Market had told the Earl that a gentleman had arrived late in the evening with two expensive carriages, each drawn by four horses.

It had not escaped the notice of curious neighbours that he had not been at Number 82 for very long before he left together with the whole household —Mrs. Carver, the servant, Hannah, and Thalia.

They had driven away without luggage, and without returning, as the Earl had at first thought they must do, to collect anything the small house contained.

It seemed to Richard even more incredible than it did to the Earl.

"Why should they have taken nothing with them?" he asked.

"Presumably because it was of no further use to them," the Earl replied. "I know that Thalia was very poor. Carriages and horses cost money. Obviously the man who called for her and her mother could afford to pay for them."

When the Earl had first been informed of the circumstances of their leaving, he had thought with a fury which he had later recognised as jealousy that Thalia had been swept away from him by some ardent lover.

Then common sense told him, when he could think about it more sanely, that it was unlikely if she was going on a romantic journey that she would have been accompanied by her mother and Hannah.

The only information the Earl had not communicated to Richard was that he had given Thalia a thousand pounds and she had returned it to him within a few hours.

That was a secret between himself and Thalia, and it merely contributed to his theory that whoever she had left with must be a rich man.

At night when he could not sleep, which he had failed dismally to do ever since he had lost Thalia, he would go over their conversations together word by word, trying to discover a clue, even the slightest hint, which might give him some idea of where she had gone.

Without this, he asked himself, how could he even begin to search the length and breadth of England for a young woman who had intrigued and mystified him ever since he had first known her?

Intent on his own problem, he was not aware that Richard regarded his behaviour first with astonishment, then with compassion.

Never in all the years he had known the Earl had he ever seen him in such a state about anything or anybody, least of all a woman.

Always in the past he had accepted them as necessities in that they could amuse and entertain him.

Never, and this was the truth, had he ever become involved so that he actively suffered from the need of one of them.

"He is in love!" Richard told himself.

But he did not say it out loud because he felt that it would only contribute further to the Earl's obvious unhappiness.

As the Earl sipped his brandy, to change the subject he asked:

"How are your horses?"

"I have no idea."

"I thought you might have been running one at Epsom."

"I believe my trainer did enquire if I wished to do so," the Earl answered vaguely.

It was obvious that his mind was elsewhere, but at that moment a Member who was passing said:

"Hello, Hellington! I expected to see you at Epsom yesterday."

The Earl merely nodded his head in recognition of the greeting, but Richard, in an effort to be polite, enquired:

"Did you have a winner?"

"Only as regards my bets," was the reply. "I withdrew my own horse."

This was obviously a sore point and the speaker moved on to sit down in a chair behind the Earl and Richard, obviously not wishing to talk any further of what had occurred.

There was a rustle of paper and then someone said:

"Good-morning, Dervish. I have not seen you for some time."

"I have been staying at Epsom," Lord Dervish replied, then in a louder tone than he had used before, he exclaimed: "Good God!"

"What has happened?"

"You will hardly believe it, but Caversham has returned the thousand pounds he owed me. It has taken him three years, and I can hardly credit it is not a joke!"

"Sir Denzil Caversham? I thought he was abroad."

"He is, but here is the thousand pounds he owed me, from his Trustees."

The Earl, who had been sitting in what Richard called to himself "the darkest gloom," suddenly sat upright.

Then to his friend's astonishment he sprang to his feet and walked to where Lord Dervish was sitting behind him.

"Forgive my intrusion, Dervish," he said, "but I could not help overhearing you saying you had received a thousand pounds from somebody after a lapse of three years."

"That is true," Lord Dervish replied. "I can tell you it is quite a shock! I never expected to see the

153

money again. In fact I intended to take out a warrant for Caversham's arrest if he ever returned to this country."

"Would you permit me to see the thousand pounds you have received?" the Earl asked.

Lord Dervish looked at him in surprise, then he said:

"I cannot see why you are interested, Hellington, unless he owes you money too. As a matter of fact, his Trustees have sent me the pounds in notes. I could not think what it was when I picked up the envelope just now when I came into the Club."

As he spoke, he held out the opened envelope and with it the letter that Thalia had written.

One glance at the writing told the Earl what he wished to know.

"Thank you," he said. "Do you happen to know Caversham's address?"

"I cannot remember it," Lord Dervish replied, "but I expect the porter can tell you. If not, he will doubtless be listed in Debrett."

"Yes, of course," the Earl said.

He turned without another word and went from the Coffee-Room, leaving Lord Dervish and Richard staring after him in perplexity.

"I do not mind betting," Lord Dervish remarked as he closed the envelope which contained the notes, "that Caversham owes Hellington a packet!"

* * *

Thalia stepped through the French window which opened onto the lawn.

As it was growing late in the afternoon the sun had lost its strength and she did not need a sunshade to prevent its rays from spoiling the whiteness of her skin.

The gardeners her father had engaged to cut away the wild growth of three years' neglect were beginning to make the garden look almost as she remembered it.

It had been a shock to see the green velvet lawns which had been there for centuries turned, as her father had said contemptuously, "into hay-fields" and the shrubs and flower-beds overgrown until they had almost a jungle-like appearance.

The house seemed to have suffered less from neglect through the years, especially as on Sir Denzil's instructions the women of the village had already removed the worst of the cob-webs and dust before they arrived.

Like a Commander directing operations in the field, Sir Denzil had begun to redecorate and refurnish the house as he and his wife had always longed to do.

Thalia lost count of the items he ordered from tradesmen who flocked to the Manor eagerly once it was known that he required their services.

It was not only that he wanted everything round him to be as fine and grand as he had always wished it to be; it was also, Thalia knew, an almost childish delight in being able to spend, spend, spend as he had never been able to do before in the whole of his life.

The story of his adventures in America left his wife and his daughter breathless, and because he was so excited about them himself, it was hard for Thalia at times not to believe that she was listening to some boy's adventure-story rather than a tale of persistence and sheer good luck.

It had been lucky that Sir Denzil had become friends, on board the ship that carried him away from England, with a man who was a prospector for gold and was in fact an expert in the field.

Sir Denzil had gone with him to Arizona, and it was due to his newfound friend that he staked the small amount of money he had with him in a prospective Gold Field that was not yet developed.

With a determination that his friends would not have expected of him, Sir Denzil worked harder, he said, than any navvy in panning gold, and was astute enough to invest every nugget he found in buying more land.

Besides the prospectors in the field, there were the riff-raff who were always looking for a "strike."

Most of them were interested in what they found only so that they could drink more with the bawdy women who were to be found in the hastily erected bars that were too sordid to attract any man who was in the least fastidious.

Gradually Sir Denzil and his partner acquired all the land that was worthwhile, and when finally they struck the deep vein they hoped for, there was no question of their ownership being in dispute.

The moment he had gained everything he required, knowing that the years of his exile were coming to an end, Sir Denzil was ready to return to New York on the first step of his journey back to England.

The Mine by this time was being worked by experts and there was nothing he and his partner could do personally but collect their profits and make sure that they would continue to flow in.

Everything was tied up extremely satisfactorily by the best Lawyers and Financial Experts in New York.

Then Sir Denzil's partner was shot by a man who believed he had defrauded him of his claim many years earlier.

The accusation was untrue, but the fact that the man was arrested did not save his victim's life.

He only just had time to make a will in Sir Denzil's favour before he died.

"I've had the greatest fun in my life these last three years that we've been together," he said to Sir Denzil. "In fact, I'd never known what it was to laugh before."

He gasped for air before he added:

"Spend my money for me, Denzil, and laugh as you do so. I shall be listening to hear you."

There were tears in Sir Denzil's eyes as he related this part of the story, and his wife held on tightly to his hand to show that she understood and wanted to comfort him.

Although the sound of her father's laughter filled the Manor and brought his wife such happiness that every day she seemed to glow with a new beauty, Thalia knew there was one part of herself that no laughter could reach.

Every night when she was alone she found herself crying helplessly for the Earl, wondering if he had forgotten her already and whether somebody like Lady Adelaide or Genevieve had taken her place in his affections.

She was certain that she had done the right thing in running away without telling him where she was going or who she was.

Although it was an agony to think there were only a few hours' fast driving between them, she could not have borne the knowledge that the Earl might believe he must behave in an honourable manner and offer her marriage.

It was not just marriage she wanted from him but something very different, and to have trapped him, for that was what it would have amounted to, into losing his freedom would, she told herself with a wry smile, have been definitely "unsporting."

"He will forget me ... of course he will forget me," she kept saying to herself, "but I will never, never forget him!"

She faced the fact that she would never love anybody else and therefore it was unlikely that she would ever marry.

It did not trouble her particularly, except that it was hard to think of the Earl without crying, and she was well aware that in some ways she was *de trop* in her own home.

Always before, she and her father had been so close and she had never wanted other companions of her own age, being utterly content to be with him.

Now something was missing between them, something she recognised as being as much his fault as hers, if fault was the right word.

His experiences in America, the tremendous effort he had had to make in an entirely different world from his own, had changed Sir Denzil from the light-hearted, rather irresponsible man he had been into a much older and wiser person.

He still retained his gift of laughter and *joie de vivre*, but he was content as he had never been before with his home, his Estate, and his wife, who adored him.

In the past he had talked to Thalia of subjects which interested him and which were outside his immediate home-life.

Now she realised, almost in surprise, that her father was middle-aged and wanted to settle down.

"Eldon was right," he said several times to his wife and daughter, "as soon as people have begun to accept me, I shall take my rightful place in County affairs. Perhaps, who knows, one day the King might appoint me to be Lord Lieutenant!"

"I hope so, darling," Lady Caversham said, "and how handsome you will look in your special uniform."

"I shall have to 'play myself in.'" Sir Denzil said. "There are a great number of Charitable Boards I must sit on first, and I must join the Yeomanry, which I should have done years ago."

He paused before he said, to please his wife:

"We must entertain, my dearest, and who will look lovelier than you at the head of the table? And of course presiding over the Ball we must give every year."

'There is really no place here for me now,' Thalia thought sadly.

She put on one of the beautiful gowns that her father had ordered for her and her mother before he bought anything else, and she could not help won-

dering what the Earl would think if he could see her in
it.

She knew it was very different from the grey
gown she had worn in the shop and from the simple
muslin in which she had dined with him.

Her new gown accentuated the perfection of her
figure and the whiteness of her skin and was a frame
for the shining glory of her hair with its touches of
fire.

A fire, Thalia thought miserably, that would never
burn in her again, whatever compliments she might
receive, whatever man's eyes looked into hers.

She walked slowly across the lawn, thinking as
she smelt the fragrance of the rose-garden that it was
still, with its weather-beaten Elizabethan brick walls
and its water-lily pool, one of the most beautiful places
she had ever seen.

'It is a place for lovers,' she thought instinctively.

Then she drew in her breath as if the thought
stabbed her physically like a sharp dagger.

She walked between the beds, crimson, white,
and pink with their roses in bloom, to stand looking
down into the water-lily pool, thinking she must remind her father to replace the gold-fish that had been
there when she was a child.

Then she asked herself what did it matter.

Gold-fish were what children loved, and she
would never have any children to try with their small
fat hands to capture the elusive little fish, nor to bring
her as she had brought her mother the first primrose of
the spring.

She knew what she wanted more than anything
else was a child who would resemble the Earl because
he was his father.

Then as the tears, never far from the surface,
came to her eyes, she felt ashamed of her own weakness.

"I will go back to the house and find something
useful to do," she told herself severely.

Barbara Cartland

As she turned she heard the footsteps of somebody walking into the rose-garden and thought it must
be her father.

Because she knew it would upset him if he saw
her in tears, she blinked her eyes to prevent them from
falling, and turned her head aside as she sought for
a handkerchief in the sash of her gown.

Several tears fell before she found it, and a voice
she had not expected to hear asked:

"You are not crying, Thalia?"

She gave a little gasp of astonishment. Then her
eyes, wide and shining with tears, looked in amaze-
ment to see the Earl standing beside her.

For a moment she thought she must be dreaming,
but there were his grey eyes holding hers captive as
he had done before, and she could only stare up at
him, feeling as if her whole body had come alive simply because he was there when she had never thought
to see him again.

"You are . . . here!" she exclaimed wonderingly.

"I am here!" he repeated. "I had almost given up
hope of ever finding you. How could you behave in such
a cruel, wicked manner? What have I ever done to
deserve such punishment?"

He spoke so sternly that her hands fluttered to her
breasts as if to control the violent beating of her heart.

Then as she knew he was waiting for an answer,
she said hesitatingly:

"I . . . I thought it was . . . best."

"For me? You have nearly destroyed me by making me suffer in thinking I had lost you forever!"

"I did not . . . mean to upset you."

"What did you expect me to feel," he asked
sharply, "when you just vanished, and I was left trying
to imagine what had happened?"

"I . . . am . . . sorry . . . terribly sorry," Thalia whispered.

She spoke humbly, yet at the same time there
160

was music in the air and the Earl seemed to be surrounded by an aura of light which was dazzling.

He was here! He was beside her and he appeared to mind that she had gone away!

She knew too that while he looked amazingly handsome, he seemed thinner and his face was more sharply drawn.

"You might at least," the Earl was saying, "have told me your real name."

"I ... did not ... wish you to ... know it."

"Why not?"

She could not tell him the real reason, and as Thalia was silent he said:

"I think you must be the only woman who would not have been curious to know what my plans for you were, the plans I told you we would talk about at dinner that night."

Thalia looked away from him as the colour rose in her cheeks.

The Earl's eyes were watching her and he thought that her straight little nose and the curve of her lips silhouetted against the roses were the loveliest things he had ever seen in his whole life.

"Have you thought about me?" he asked unexpectedly.

"O-of course I ... have!"

"And have you wondered what I was going to suggest to you when we dined together?"

It was impossible to answer and after a moment he said:

"I had a present for you."

"You ... know I would not have accepted a ... present after what you had ... given me already."

"I told you that the one thousand pounds, which I know now was for your father, did not concern us. The present I was going to give you was something very different."

"I am ... sorry I had to ... miss ... receiving it."

161

"I will give it to you now."

She turned her head to look up at him.

There was an expression in his eyes which made her heart beat even more violently than it was already.

"I am afraid that since I have taken so long in finding you, it is somewhat out-of-date."

The Earl drew something from the inside pocket of his closely fitting coat as he spoke.

It was a piece of paper and as Thalia took it from him she wondered what it could be.

It was difficult to think of anything except the Earl himself, but because he was waiting she opened the paper, then stared at it in astonishment.

It was a Marriage-Certificate made out in the name of Vargus Alexander Mark, fifth Earl of Hellington, bachelor, and Thalia Carver, spinster!

For a moment she could hardly believe what she saw, then an inexpressible joy swept over her.

He wanted to marry her! He loved her enough to want her not as his mistress but as his wife, even though she had been nothing more than a shop-assistant!

The Marriage-Certificate trembled in her hand and she was aware that the Earl had drawn a little closer, so close that their bodies were almost touching, as he said:

"Perhaps Miss Caversham feels differently from Miss Thalia Carver, whom I very distinctly remember saying that she loved me."

"I . . . I did not wish you to . . . feel that I was . . . trying to . . . catch you," Thalia stammered.

"I was caught already," the Earl replied, "caught, and completely hooked for all time."

He took the Marriage-Certificate from her and threw it onto the ground. Then he pulled her into his arms, holding her so close against him that it was hard to breathe.

"Will you marry me, my darling? I cannot live without you!"

He did not wait for her answer, but his lips sought hers.

As he kissed her, Thalia knew again that wonder and glory he had given her before when he had carried her up to the stars and they hung suspended there with all the problems of the world far away below them.

She felt as if the Earl made her his and they were indivisible, and yet it was something they had been since they first knew each other.

They belonged, they were one, and she had never thought that what he felt for her could be the same as what she felt for him.

Now she knew how much he wanted and needed her and she felt her whole mind and body respond in a manner which told her they could never be divided.

Their love was greater than time or space or any man-made divisions of class or status.

"I love ... you! I love ... you!" she whispered as the Earl released her lips.

She was trembling with the ecstasy he had evoked in her and she thought he was trembling too.

"I love you and you will never leave me again!" he replied. "I could not bear it."

Then he was kissing her wildly, passionately, demandingly, and a fire leapt within them both until Thalia seemed to break under the strain of it and hid her face against his shoulder.

"How soon will you marry me?" he asked, and his voice was deep and unsteady.

"As soon as ... you ... want me to ... do so."

"That is now—this moment!"

She gave a little cry of sheer happiness.

"I was so ... certain that you had no wish to ... marry anybody."

"I only want to marry you. There has never been another woman who made me feel as you do or made me realise I could never be happy without her."

"And ... suppose you find ... once we are married

. . . that you are . . .bored with me, as you have . . been with so many . . . other women?"

The Earl's arms tightened round her.

"I became bored with other women because they were not you," he said. "This is different, my precious love, and it will take me a very long time to tell you how different."

He looked down at her, then held her from him at arm's length.

"I have never seen you fashionably gowned before."

"Do you . . . like me like . . . this?"

"I love you whatever you wear," he replied, "but I am disappointed."

"D-disappointed?" Thalia asked anxiously.

"I wanted to give you the right background for your beauty and I used to imagine how different you would look without that little grey gown. But now your father has had the fun that I had promised myself."

"It has not . . . spoilt things for . . . you?"

The Earl smiled.

"Nothing would do that. It is just that I want you to belong to me so completely and absolutely and to know there is nobody in your life except me."

"There is . . . no-one in my life . . . except you."

She saw the delight her words brought to his eyes.

Then as if she felt she must reassure him, she moved closer to him.

"It is . . . hard to believe you are . . . here," she said. "I have . . . missed you so . . . desperately . . . I have been so terribly . . . unhappy without you . . . and I thought I should be . . . alone for the rest of my life."

She knew he understood what she meant by the word "alone," and he said with his lips touching the softness of her cheek:

"That is what I felt. It was as if you took part of me away with you and I knew I would never be complete again until I had found you."

He made a sound that was half a laugh and half a groan.

"I never knew that love could be so painful, such excruciating misery."

"And . . . now?"

"Now it is a wonder beyond words, a happiness which-I believe, my darling, will grow every day and every year that we are together."

He drew her closer still before he said:

"There is no end to our love—yours and mine—it is something which Fate brought to us and Fate will never take away. I will love you, my beautiful one, from now until eternity, and that will not be long enough for me."

"That is . . . how I . . . love you."

Thalia gave a little cry as she raised her lips to his.

"Make me . . . sure this is . . . true! Make me . . . sure I am not . . . dreaming," she begged. "It is so wonderful . . . so absolutely . . . wonderful . . . as you are."

It was impossible for her to say any more, for the Earl's lips were on hers.

She knew that everything they were trying to put into words was expressed in his kiss, which seemed to come from the sun itself and which enveloped them with the dazzling, blinding light that was Divine.

ABOUT THE AUTHOR

BARBARA CARTLAND, the world's most famous romantic novelist, who is also an historian, playwright, lecturer, political speaker and television personality, has now written over 200 books.

She has also had many historical works published and has written four autobiographies as well as the biographies of her mother and that of her brother Ronald Cartland, who was the first Member of Parliament to be killed in the last war. This book has a preface by Sir Winston Churchill.

Barbara Cartland has sold 100 million books over the world, more than half of these in the U.S.A. She broke the world record in 1975 by writing twenty books, and her own record in 1976 with twenty-one. In addition, her album of love songs has just been published, sung with the Royal Philharmonic Orchestra.

In private life, Barbara Cartland, who is a Dame of the Order of St. John of Jerusalem, has fought for better conditions and salaries for Midwives and Nurses. As President of the Royal College of Midwives (Hertfordshire Branch), she has been invested with the first Badge of Office ever given in Great Britain which was subscribed to by the Midwives themselves. She has also championed the cause for old people and founded the first Romany Gypsy Camp in the world.

Barbara Cartland is deeply interested in Vitamin Therapy and is President of the British National Association for Health.

Barbara Cartland

The world's bestselling author of romantic fiction.
Her stories are always captivating tales of intrigue,
adventure and love.

☐ 12572	THE DRUMS OF LOVE	$1.50
☐ 12576	ALONE IN PARIS	$1.50
☐ 12638	THE PRINCE AND THE PEKINGESE	$1.50
☐ 12637	A SERPENT OF SATAN	$1.50
☐ 12273	THE TREASURE IS LOVE	$1.50
☐ 12785	THE LIGHT OF THE MOON	$1.50
☐ 12792	PRISONER OF LOVE	$1.50
☐ 12281	FLOWERS FOR THE GOD OF LOVE	$1.50
☐ 12654	LOVE IN THE DARK	$1.50
☐ 13036	A NIGHTINGALE SANG	$1.50
☐ 13035	LOVE CLIMBS IN	$1.50
☐ 12962	THE DUCHESS DISAPPEARED	$1.50
☐ 13126	TERROR IN THE SUN	$1.50
☐ 13330	WHO CAN DENY LOVE?	$1.50
☐ 13364	LOVE HAS HIS WAY	$1.50

Bantam Book Catalog

Here's your up-to-the-minute listing of over 1,400 titles by your favorite authors.

This illustrated, large format catalog gives a description of each title. For your convenience, it is divided into categories in fiction and non-fiction—gothics, science fiction, westerns, mysteries, cookbooks, mysticism and occult, biographies, history, family living, health, psychology, art.

So don't delay—take advantage of this special opportunity to increase your reading pleasure.

Just send us your name and address and 50¢ (to help defray postage and handling costs).